500

FACES IN THE WATER

Books by Phyllis Reynolds Naylor

Witch's Sister
Witch Water
The Witch Herself
Walking Through the Dark
How I Came to Be a Writer
How Lazy Can You Get?
Eddie, Incorporated
All Because I'm Older
Shadows on the Wall
Faces in the Water
Footprints at the Window
The Boy with the Helium Head
A String of Chances
The Solomon System
Bernie Magruder & the Case of the Big Stink
Night Cry
Old Sadie and the Christmas Bear
The Dark of the Tunnel
The Agony of Alice
The Keeper
Bernie Magruder & the Haunted Hotel
The Year of the Gopher
Beetles, Lightly Toasted
Maudie in the Middle
One of the Third Grade Thonkers
Alice in Rapture, Sort Of
Keeping a Christmas Secret
Bernie Magruder & the Disappearing Bodies
Send No Blessings
Reluctantly Alice

FACES IN THE WATER

PHYLLIS REYNOLDS NAYLOR

Aladdin Paperbacks

NEW YORK LONDON TORONTO SYDNEY SINGAPORE

First Aladdin Paperbacks edition February 2002
Copyright © 1981 by Phyllis Reynolds Naylor
Aladdin Paperbacks
An imprint of Simon & Schuster
Children's Publishing Division
1230 Avenue of the Americas
New York, NY 10020

The Library of Congress has cataloged the hardcover edition as follows:
Naylor, Phyllis Reynolds.
Faces in the Water
The second vol. of a trilogy; the first is Shadows on the Wall.
Summary: During Daniel's summer visit with his grandmother in York County,
Pennsylvania, characters and events from his visit to York, England, appear and
reappear in mysterious ways.
ISBN 0-689-30823-X
[1.Space and time—Fiction. 2.England—Fiction. 3.Pennsylvania—Fiction]
I. Title.
PZ7.N24Fac [Fic] 80-24057
ISBN 0-689-84962-1 (Aladdin pbk.)

To Jeff & Michael in the months ahead

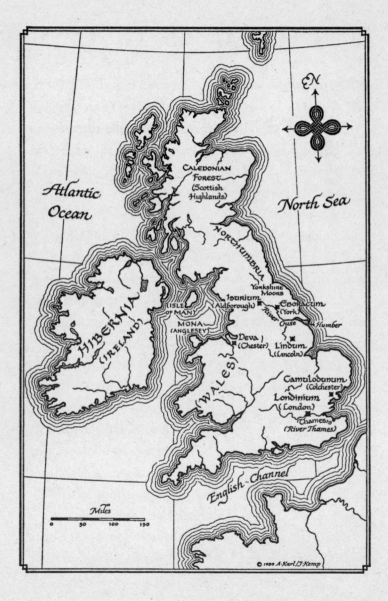

North

Atlantic
Ocean

North Sea

CALEDONIAN
FOREST
(Scottish
Highlands)

NORTHUMBRIA

Yorkshire
Moors

HIBERNIA
(IRELAND)

ISLE
OF MAN

ISURIUM
Aldborough

EBORACUM
(York)

River Ouse

Humber

MONA
(ANGLESEY)

Deva
(Chester)

LINDUM
(Lincoln)

WALES

CAMULODUNUM
(Colchester)

LONDINIUM
(London)

Thamesis
(River Thames)

English Channel

Miles

0   50   100   150

© 1980 A·Karl / J·Kemp

PROLOGUE

Somewhere west of Albany, hidden in the Catskills, there is a small lake called Otsego. From this lake springs the Susquehanna River, flowing southward. On through the Alleghenies it winds, till it takes an eastward turn and empties, at last, into Chesapeake Bay.

Once its banks were known only to the Susquehannocks Indians, and the river waited, biding its time, while colonists settled along the coast. It laughed as a swaggering Captain John Smith attempted to row up its channel in 1608, only to be stopped by a bristling barrier of jagged boulders. On the river tumbled, knowing that some day other men would try to conquer it too—the strong, the weak, the upright, the wayward, the wise, the foolish. . . .

In 1630, a different sort of man migrated to America— a prosperous shipyard owner and hotel proprietor from Colchester, England. Perhaps he had plans to navigate the rivers, to build lodgings for travelers on their banks, to make for his children a new home in a new place. But Nathaniel Welles left for his descendants a legacy of another kind; he carried a gene responsible for a hereditary disorder now known as Huntington's disease.

Three other men with the defective gene also left England that year and sailed to America. Many of their relatives had behaved strangely and committed various crimes. Their communities did not understand them, and some of the women were burned at the stake as witches.

These men, then—Nathaniel Welles, William Knapp, and Geoffrey and Nicholas Haste—came seeking a refuge. They sired children, and slowly—as their descendants married and intermarried—the disease spread, first in New England, then into other parts of the country.

The Susquehanna has known them all—the wanderers, the afflicted, the saints, the cowards, the courageous—all have settled on its banks and tried to tame it, for the river is swift, its bed shallow, and its path obstructed with rocks. Concealed beneath its waters are currents that travel unrecognized channels from ancient generations to our own.

As the river passes through southern Pennsylvania, it divides the town of Mt. Joy on one side from Mt. Wolf on the other. It is here in this place that the story continues.

I

"The universe is change; our life is what our thoughts make it."

—Marcus Aurelius Antoninus [A.D. 121–180]

IT WAS ALWAYS the edge of dawn when he heard it. The sky was never quite black, never quite gray, never streaked with pink or silver, and yet the crack was there—the invisible seam that separated things of the night from the colors of day. It was at this time, for almost a week now, that Dan had heard someone calling his name.

It was more of a rasp than a whisper, and it came raucously through the walls of his room like a ripping of plaster. There was something inhuman about the sound. Each time, Dan would raise his head from the pillow and say, "What?" and then, still louder, "What is it?" But the answer never came. As soon as his name was spoken, silence swallowed it up.

He was not afraid, exactly—not yet. The voice did not spawn the clammy dread that Dan had experienced a month before in York. It was more a vague uneasiness that somehow he had been followed.

He sat up and swung his legs over the edge of the bed. He would sleep no more, he knew. The voice called only once each morning, but it left him restless. If he ignored it, would it go away, becoming softer and softer till at last it was nothing? Or would it, enraged at his inattention, be emboldened enough to take on shape and substance?

Whatever, he decided not to seek it out. He was through with things of the past that he had unwittingly summoned in May. When he returned home from York, in fact, he had taken the small Roman coin that Nat had given him and thrust it quickly into an inner pocket of his wallet, intent on selling it the next time he went downtown.

Now he jerked his head suddenly and listened. There were footsteps outside his room—pausing, then moving on. Despite his resolution to let things be, he crept to the door and suddenly flung it open.

"Lord, Dan! You gave me a start!"

His father stood there in his robe, unshaven. "What are you doing up at this hour?"

"Seeing who else is up," Dan said, looking a little sheepish.

"Well, come on out to the kitchen. I'll make hot cakes if you'll squeeze the oranges."

They sat together at the table, each looking at the other when he thought he was unobserved. If there was anything that upset Dan now, it was this chronic, compulsive spying: Dan, to see if there was anything abnormal about his father, and Mr. Roberts, to see if Dan was checking.

They knew what it was all about, however—had even promised to stop. Since coming back from York, Dan had turned sixteen and was determined to act more mature, be more accepting. But the watching, they knew, would go on the rest of their lives unless the thing they both feared came true—unless Dan's father showed symptoms of Huntington's disease. Then the suspense would be over, for Mr. Roberts, at least.

If his father did have it—if he had inherited the gene from his own father—Dan had a fifty percent chance of having it, too. If Mr. Roberts showed none of the symptoms, however, it didn't necessarily prove a thing. Not until his father was fifty or sixty—seventy, even—and without symptoms could Dan assume that the chain had been broken forever. Only then could he think about having children of his own. Catch 22: if he waited long enough to be sure, it would be too late. You didn't wait till you were forty to think about getting married and playing baseball with your kids. And if his father died early of something else, Dan would never know at all whether or not he might have it.

A miracle, that's what he wanted. A cure. At the very least a test that would detect Huntington's disease early, long before there were symptoms, something to end the uncertainty. But there was no reliable test—not yet, anyway. And if there were, and he carried the gene, would he really want to know? He wasn't sure. And so the watching went on.

"Have you thought any more about going to your grandmother's this summer?" Mr. Roberts asked, picking up hotcakes one at a time with the spatula and slowly, almost too carefully, transferring them to Dan's plate.

"I'd rather get a job here, but it looks pretty hopeless. Bill's been looking since March—finally took a Saturday job washing cars."

"Grandma Bee could use your help," his father continued. It was "B" for Blossom, Sara Blossom, actually, but over the years she'd simply become Grandma Bee.

"I thought she hired somebody."

"To mow the fields and milk the cow, but she's still got the garden and house to contend with. She's getting up in years—lonely. Like to have you around, I know."

It was not that Dan did not want to go. He liked his father's mother—liked the two-hundred-year-old house she lived in with a spring bubbling up through the earthen floor of the cellar, flowing out an open space in one wall. He liked the little town of Mt. Joy also, on down the river from Harrisburg. But he was reluctant to leave his parents now, even though there was nothing he could do to help. It was just better being a part of it, sharing it with them. Yet the uncertainty could go on for years, and it was this that gnawed away at him, squeezing his heart and filling his lungs with ice water.

Dan slathered syrup over his hot cakes and passed the pitcher to his father. He had just picked up his fork when he noticed the strange way his dad's hand was shaking. A thin coil of syrup dribbled down onto the tablecloth.

"Damn nerves!" Mr. Roberts said, and went to get a wet cloth.

Back in his room, Dan pulled on his jeans and reached in the closet for his belt with the eagle buckle before remembering that he had traded it to Nat. He chose another and thrust it through his belt loops.

He had to get away for a while. It was no good, the watching. They'd drive each other nuts at this rate and wouldn't need Huntington's disease to do them in. Okay, he would go to Mt. Joy for a few weeks, just to give himself and his dad a rest.

Suddenly he whirled about, sure that he had heard his name again. He went over to the window and looked out into the misty half-light. He saw nothing but the linden tree and then, on its lowest branch, a black bird.

✳ ✳ ✳

Dan stood on the front steps waiting for Bill, travel bag beside him.

"Tell him thanks for driving you to the bus station," Dan's mother said, coming out the door with her notebook and text. "It's going to be a hectic summer, my being in school and only one car between us." She paused. "I think it will be good for you to get away for a while, Dan. Good for Grandma Bee—for all of us."

He nodded, and she fumbled with the keys, but made no move toward the car. "Dad's under a lot of pressure, you know. This whole thing is getting him down. He says he won't go on worrying about it forever, but. . . . Well, it's hard not to. Waiting for something's the worst."

"Yeah, I know." Dan wondered if he should mention the way his father's hand had been shaking the other morning at breakfast. Perhaps she'd already noticed.

"I don't want you going back to school in the fall feeling as though you haven't had any summer, any fun."

Dan smiled. "Hey, we had York, remember? I've had a month of vacation already. It was great."

She looked relieved. "I'm glad. We all enjoyed it—something to remember. Well. . . ." She started down the steps, came back up and hugged him, then went down again. "You won't get bored at Mt. Joy, will you? If you do, you can always come back. It's not as though we're trying to get rid of you or anything. . . ."

"I've got that article to write for Bill. He wants it for the first issue in September. That'll give me plenty to do, just deciphering my notes."

"Good. It will be nice to see it in print." She flung her arm out dramatically. "A part of our trip immortalized forever."

They laughed—politely—and she got in the car, backing it down the drive.

Dan sat on the top step to wait for his friend. He had not had a chance to tell Bill all he would have liked. Since he'd returned from York, the newspaper staff had been frantic in its race to sell ads to the local merchants before other schools got to them first. The size of next year's paper depended on the number of sales. Consequently, any conversation between Dan and Bill, who was editor-in-chief, was likely to be, "Did you get around any this week?" "Where'd you go?" "How much?" He smiled to himself. This was journalism? For this he was going to slave through college?

As Bill's old Buick turned in the drive, Dan had a sudden impulse to tell him more about York: about Joe Stanton and the gypsy, about what he had experienced that night on the moor. This was neither the time nor the place, but still he felt that he should. Someone ought to know, in case. . . .

Bill was shorter than Dan, a little on the stocky side,

and red-haired down to the eyelashes. He drove casually, two fingers resting on the wheel, one beat-up sneaker on the gas pedal. "I'll probably get you there too early," he said, "but the car's been going in fits and starts, so I wanted to allow extra time."

"That's okay. I'm enjoying the company," Dan told him.

"How's the story coming? What'd you call it—'A Gypsy Burial' or something?"

"Yeah. I think it'll work. Should have it to you by August."

"Great."

Dan sat staring out the side window. Now? Should he tell him now? Should he just say, *Bill, something really weird happened to me in York this spring. There were these Roman soldiers, see. . . . ?*

"Bill, something really weird happened to me in York this spring." The words were out before he knew it.

"Yeah? What?"

"I had a strange experience. You may not believe it—"

"What was it? What happened?"

"There's a story, see, about the cellar of the Treasurer's House in York. Four different people have seen ghosts of Roman soldiers there. It's a fact that the very wall of the cellar from which they came is the location of the entrance of the old Roman garrison."

Bill looked at him, his red eyebrows raised curiously. "Yeah? Did you see them?"

"Not in the cellar. Out on the moor. The night the gypsy grandmother was buried."

Bill continued staring at him: "So what happened?"

"They were . . . marching through the camp. And one of them wrestled with me. I don't know what it was all about. He didn't try to use his weapons. Just chased me up a hill, and we grappled around on the ground. And then . . . then he became somebody else—Joe Stanton, the cab driver. He was as surprised as I was."

Bill shook his head. "I don't think you know a nightmare when you have one."

It was, Dan decided, the only reaction he could expect. He knew, even as he'd said the words, how fantastic it sounded. If Bill had told *him* the story, would he have believed it? Not a chance.

"It wasn't a dream, Bill. I sat up there on the hill with Joe and we talked about it afterwards. He was frightened, too. But he's seen them before, he says, the soldiers. . . ."

Bill frowned and continued driving.

Dan waited. Finally, when the silence became unbearable, he snapped, "Well, for Pete's sake, *say* something. Don't just look away like you're pretending I'm not here—like you're driving me off to the looney farm or something."

Bill glanced at him quickly. "Hey, easy! I don't know *what* to say, that's all. Gad, you throw something like this and expect me to say something profound?"

Dan leaned back against the seat and closed his eyes. "Yeah, I know. It sounds weird, really weird. I haven't even told my folks. It took all this time to get up the nerve to tell you."

They had reached the bus station. Bill switched off the engine and turned, facing Dan. "So why are you telling me now?"

"I don't know. I have this premonition, I guess, that something might happen."

"To you?"

"Maybe."

"In Mt. Joy? At your grandmother's?"

"Yes."

"Listen, Dan, do you really think it's smart to be going? Maybe you ought to stay here and get your head together."

"See a shrink, you mean?"

Bill shrugged. "A shrink, a family doctor . . . whatever. You've been all keyed up since you got back from England, you know it? Tense, serious. . . ."

"It's all in the head, then. Is that what you think?"

"Look. I know you're not the sort of person who goes around imagining things. I know that if any of the other guys on the staff had told you the story you just told me,

10

you'd ask for proof. So it's not like you to invent some-thing. Maybe you *did* see Roman soldiers. And maybe they're making a wreck of you. Just because I can't explain something doesn't mean it didn't happen. You just haven't been yourself, though. It's like somebody wound you up, and you just can't stop." He let out his breath and thought for a moment, drumming his fingers against the wheel. "I don't know—maybe a couple weeks in the country is the best thing after all."

Dan felt strangely relieved that he had told someone, though nothing much had come of it. "It sounds as nutty to me as it does to you. But it happened."

"Okay, it happened. You going to write about it then, for the paper?"

Dan shook his head. "I'll stick to the gypsy burial and let it go at that." He picked up his bag from the back and slid it over the seat. "Thanks, Bill. Take care."

"August, then?" Bill called after him. His voice was casual, but he watched Dan intently. "I can count on it? We want to get the paper out the first week of school—drum up school spirit, customers."

"You got it. Save me a whole page."

Mt. Joy, named after an Irish ship in 1689, the good ship Mountjoy, nestled near the Susquehanna, connected to it by a stream. When the river was low, large rocks—like stepping stones for giants—surfaced above the water. But when the river was high, rushing dark and tumultuous toward the bay and the ocean beyond, many of the rocks lay submerged, awaiting the careless boatman who would venture out.

The surrounding countryside was rich in lime and heavily populated with the Amish and Mennonite farmers who had tended their crops generation after generation, son following father and grandfather. A sense of history hung about the place as surely as the heady smell of clover or of earth, freshly plowed. Somewhere among these homes sat the old stone house of Blossom Roberts.

She had told Dan that she was sending the hired man to meet him, and as the bus pulled over at the stop, Dan could see her gray station wagon parked on the shoulder of the highway further up. He pulled his bag off the shelf above the seat, looped the sleeves of his sweatshirt around his neck, and stepped off.

He walked along the road toward the car, marveling at the quiet. The frenetic selling of ads, the compiling of the first issue of the school paper, the eternal hunt for summer jobs, his mother's classes, his father's restlessness and worry. . . . All these he had left behind him. It was as though he were setting foot in a new land, where he could be someone else. Was it a cop-out, he wondered? Should he have come?

He reached Bee's station wagon, opened the rear door and slung his bag into the back, then opened the front and slid in beside the driver. Instantly his body froze, his throat constricted, and a wave of terror washed over him, for he seemed to be staring into the very eyes of Jasper Faw— elder son of the gypsy.

Whether the young man recognized him too or was simply reacting to the shock on his face, Dan couldn't tell, but for a moment they each tensed—motionless—as though caught in the flash of a strobe light. And then, just as suddenly, the civilized necessities took over, and each extended a hand.

"You must be Lonnie," Dan said, watching him closely. Was it his eyes that were so like Jasper's, their furtiveness? The line of the jaw? The slump of the shoulders, perhaps, or the mustache? Or did he only imagine it all? Lonnie certainly seemed older than Jasper—twenty-four, perhaps. But the resemblance was uncanny.

The young man nodded and started the engine, eyes on the rearview mirror. "Bee—she hired me two weeks ago. Said you was coming today. I figured you'd know her car, so I just stayed put."

"That's okay."

The car moved back onto the highway. The white fence posts that lined the road came on, one after another, in stately procession—vertical columns of white as far as the eye could see. Dan tried to keep his attention focused on the posts—tried not to stare at the person beside him.

"Live around here, Lonnie?"

"About."

Dan waited. "Not from Mt. Joy, though, are you?"

Lonnie shook his head. "No. I follow the river—go wherever there's work." He looked at Dan, facing him directly. "Keep thinking I've seen you before."

Dan gave it a wild shot: "How about last spring, out on the moor?"

"Where's that?"

The question was so honest and direct that Dan was reassured for the moment and felt foolish for bringing it up. "Oh, it's a long way off," he said. "I guess I just have one of those common faces."

Lonnie smiled, his eyes on the road again. "I don't know. It's a way with me—always seeing things I've seen before, but never connecting 'em. Ma says it's a gift—says maybe I've seen 'em in a dream, and if only I'd put my mind to it, I'd get premonitions and things, like those folks who predict for the newspapers and everybody waits to see if it comes true. But I'm not sure I'd want to know."

Again, the resemblance to the Faws was unnerving.

"You live with your mother, then?"

"There's a tribe of us—was, anyway, till Gabe went off. Dad, Ma, a brother, two sisters. . . ."

14

Dan listened, his skin cold. The Faws exactly.

The car came to a stop in the grassy clearing at the end of the lane. The two-story house stood heavy and thick there among the sycamore trees, and already Dan could hear the faint trickle of water as the stream flowed out through one wall of the cellar and ran down the hill to the creek.

Bee came bustling out in a lavender dress with a rose pinned to the bosom in honor of Dan's arrival. She had soft slippers on her feet and tugged at the braid of white hair at the nape of her neck, pinning it into place.

Dan always expected her to have aged some more when he saw her, but she never seemed to, except for her hands, which were arthritic and getting worse. She had the same faded blue eyes, same thin lips, same tissue-paper skin over the temples, revealing the veins beneath.

She gave up fussing with her hair and put out both arms to welcome him.

"Hey, Bee! You get younger, I swear it! Down to fifty-nine now, aren't you?"

"Bosh!" She gave him a wet kiss and grabbed his arm tightly. "First time I've put eyes on you since you went flying over the ocean! Begun to think you'd all abandoned me."

"Ha! Fat chance!" Dan teased. "You'd send the Marines." They laughed.

As Dan turned toward the car for his bag, he noticed that Lonnie was heading over to the stream beside the house. He knelt there on the ground, cupping his hands for a drink, then splashed the cold water over his face, wiping it on his sleeve. The water looked so inviting that Dan too went over, remembering the special mineral taste of it. No sooner had his lips touched the water than he heard the call again: "Dan."

It seemed far off, as though coming from the woods beyond the south pasture. Dan stood up and looked but could see no one, nothing. When he turned back again, however, Lonnie was watching intently, the deepset eyes fixed on him as though taking readings of his mind. Dan hurried back to the car, picked up his bag, and went on inside.

They sat across from each other that evening having tea in china cups in the front parlor, which smelled of dust and the mildewed pages of old books. It was Blossom's idea of a proper welcome. The cups would be put away after tonight, Dan knew, and not brought out until there were guests again. The large sand-colored cat lay on the sofa smiling a wide cat smile, its head resting against Dan's thigh.

The rose that Grandma Bee had pinned to her dress that afternoon was fading, but her eyes were still lively.

She sat with both feet on the floor, pushing herself back and forth in the rocker, as though to ward off darkness and sleep.

Dan talked on, telling her about England and the food and the beds and the trains and the wall around York with its separate gateways. He talked about Joe Stanton and Ambrose Faw and the green and gold *vardo*, but he did not tell her about the old gypsy granny's burial out on the moor.

Blossom watched him, and Dan sensed a slowing down of her rocking. "So you have told me about the young ones and the middle-aged ones," she said at last, "but you haven't told me what happened to the old granny that you wrote about from York."

"She was sick when I left," he said, hedging the truth.

"And. . . . ?"

Dan didn't answer. He lifted his cup to his lips once more, then realized that the tea was gone.

"So she died, did she?" The rocking resumed again, and Blossom clicked her teeth in time to the squeaking of the chair. "For seventy-seven years I have watched the seasons. I have seen things born, seen them die, seen them reborn again in the spring." She leaned forward and looked directly into Dan's face, her voice mischievous. "And suddenly, in my advancing years, nobody talks about death anymore." She laughed then, and her laughter broke the tension in the room. "Well, it will come whether we talk about it or not. Now, what did the old granny die of?"

"Joe Stanton thought it was appendicitis. He wanted to take her to the hospital, but she wouldn't hear of it."

"And can't say that I blame her, either," Blossom said. "Why, when I broke my hip a few years back, the hospital was the only place I couldn't get me a decent night's sleep. They wake you at five to take your temperature, they wake you again at six to take your blood pressure, and at night, just after you've gone to sleep, they wake you to give you a sleeping pill. Now how's a body to get well, I ask you?"

Dan laughed and rested his head on the back of the sofa, legs stretched out before him. If it were winter, there would have been a fire in the hearth. Instead, the screenless windows were open and a breeze fluttered in, sweeping across the room into the front hallway and out the window in Bee's bedroom on the other side.

"We keep worrying about you, being here by yourself, though," he told her. "The dampness of this house—it just can't be good for your arthritis. You know that."

"Of course I know that. But the city can't be good for my heart, and if I had to give up my house—the house I've had for sixty-one years, now—my heart would be the first to go."

Dan smiled at her fondly. "Okay. I did my duty. Mom wanted me to be sure to ask if you wouldn't consider moving into a condominium or something."

18

"Ha!" The word shot out of Blossom's mouth in a shower of spittle. "Don't talk to me of condominiums, boy—everybody living smack dab up against the next, every apartment just like the one beside it, Muzak in the elevator, a community pool. I've not enough gypsy blood in me to live out under the stars like that Yorkshire granny, perhaps, but I'm gypsy enough to want to live my own way without a set of rules posted in the activity room."

"What do you mean—gypsy blood? I never knew you had any gypsy in you at all."

Did he only imagine it, Dan wondered, or did her eyes narrow just a bit, her lips set, her face become more cautious?

"Well, I'm old enough, I guess, that I don't have to keep secrets," she said. "Yes, there's a bit of the traveler in me, but I never wanted your grandfather to know it. Was afraid he'd think I was low-born." She laughed heartily, remembering. "Silly of me, wasn't it? Seems so now. But there *was* a gypsy in my background. My great-grandfather, he was. Some said he was an Irish tinker, and some said he was a Scot. My mother said he could have been either, since he traveled about all over the place, through one country and into the next."

"Is that why you hired Lonnie?" Dan asked. "The gypsy in you, the traveler in him?"

She smiled. "Yes, I suppose it is. Every summer there's

some migrants going through, and when they ask for work, I'll not say no."

"But you don't really know much about Lonnie, do you, Bee?"

Blossom grunted disgustedly. "Now don't *you* start. When your father called me last week he says, 'Mother, what do you know about that man?' Everybody expects to find him run off some morning and me in the kitchen with a knife in my back. And what's he to take, I ask you? What's there to rob an old woman of but her life? And why would he want mine, when he's young and has life enough of his own?" She rocked furiously back and forth for a minute or two.

"But you need someone permanent, Bee."

"Then I'll get me somebody after he's gone."

There was potato salad left over from dinner and no room in Bee's refrigerator for it. She shuffled about the kitchen in her slippers as she cleaned up for the night, clicking her tongue at the bowl on the table.

"Take it down to the cellar for me, would you, Dan, and set it there in the stream? Won't do to let it get warm and make us both sick now, will it?" ·

Dan opened the door to the cellar, then remembered that there was no light below. He could never understand why, when Bee had the house wired, she had not installed electricity in either cellar or attic.

Because I don't sit me down there of an evening and read the paper now, do I? A lantern works just as well, she had told him once when he'd asked.

"Wait," Blossom said, and gave him the lantern.

Holding the lamp in his other hand, Dan went down the narrow stairs, and the bubbling of the spring grew louder. The smell of damp earth, of mold, of ancient stone embedded in moss filled his nostrils—a familiar smell, a good smell he had known since childhood. How often he had taken off his shoes on a hot summer day and gone to the cellar to wade in the stream, making little boats of paper, which went sailing out the hole in one wall and rushing down to the creek and the Susquehanna beyond.

The spring bubbled up from a crevice in the rocky floor, and Dan leaned over it and drank. As he lifted his head, he was conscious of a shadow moving on the opposite wall. He turned quickly to see who was there. Standing up, he took the lantern and examined every foot of the cellar, behind every barrel, in every space. There was no one. Nothing. He set the bowl in the shallow water as Bee had directed, took one more look around, and went back up to the kitchen.

2

ORNINGS were clear and breezy, but by afternoon, a haze hung over the valley, and creatures that had frolicked in the pasture only hours before stood listless, the sun burning through their coats.

In the heat of the day, Dan took refuge in the wood where the spring water joined Little Donegal Creek as it made its winding passage to the Susquehanna. He liked the feel of being enveloped by liquid coolness, for his arms were always tired and his shoulders ached. But he felt a strange contentment here in this place, away from Harrisburg, and he enjoyed working with his hands, his back, his muscles.

Lonnie, too, came to the woods to refresh himself, but his comings and goings never coincided with Dan's. The two moved in syncopated rhythm and kept their distance.

When he hoed the garden at the side of Bee's house, Dan could see out over the field where Lonnie was working. Sometimes he imagined that the lone figure there on the mower was watching him too, but the face was shadowed beneath the straw hat. The young man with the faint mustache had said very little since the day Dan arrived. He checked in with Bee in the early morning, before Dan was even up, and came back to the house about noon for lunch.

They sat outside when it was clear, under the beech tree—Bee on a bench at the table, Dan and Lonnie sprawled on the grass, soaking up the coolness of the earth. There was no compulsion to talk; they were often too tired for that. Usually it was Bee saying, "Sky's clouding up some in the south; might rain before long," or "Ever notice how the starlings go in one side of the barn and come out the other?" And Dan and Lonnie would glance in the direction she was pointing without answering.

Bee did not try to force their friendship. She never suggested, when Dan went for a swim in the creek, that Lonnie might enjoy it too. When Lonnie stood in the kitchen doorway and wanted to know if there was anything she needed from town, Bee never asked Dan if he'd like to ride along. She accepted both their need to talk and their need for silence, though their talk was mostly to her.

There was a letter from Dan's mother on Wednesday,

and with it, included but not opened, a letter addressed to Dan from Joe Stanton. Dan sat down on his bed to read them:

Dear Dan:

This letter came from Mr. Stanton. I think it's nice of him to keep in touch. He wrote me also, to thank us for the book we sent him. We were so fortunate to have met him while we were in York.

Please don't be alarmed, but your father's going into the hospital next week for some tests. I'm sure you must have noticed Brian's hand trembling—that and his sleeplessness. It's possible that the tests won't really tell us anything conclusive, but then again, maybe they will.

In any case, there's no need for you to cut your visit short with Grandma Bee; there's nothing you can do here. We've got to learn to live with this uncertainty, so please stay with Bee as long as you feel you can. It means a lot to her. I promise to let you know immediately if there's any more news about Dad.

Love,
Mother

Dan could feel the tension beginning at the back of his neck, but there was a certain relief in knowing that at last something was happening, that somebody was doing something, that someone might finally give them an answer.

He lay back on the bed, staring up at the printed wallpaper, the copper lamp, and the picture of a ship—a sinking ship, to be precise—above the bureau. What if they got the answer, and the news was bad? What then? Was it better not to know, so that you could hope, or was certainty always preferable to maybe?

Slowly he ran his finger under the flap of the smaller envelope with Joe Stanton's return address in the upper corner.

The handwriting was unique—a tall, slender backhand with wide loops on the R's and T's:

Dear Dan:

I have regretted that we were both exhausted when we said goodbye in York. I don't suppose that you have made sense of what happened anymore than I. But I trust that your return to the states has broken whatever connection you had with the Roman soldiers, and that you will remember me with kindness when you think of York.

Ambrose Faw has a request, which is the real intent of this letter. It seems that Nat traded you an ancient Roman coin for your belt when you were there. I have assured Ambrose that it was undoubtedly at Nat's urging that the exchange was made, and that you would not have agreed to it had you known its history.

The old granny had a small bag of gold and silver coins,

which had been passed down to her by her grandfather and who knows how many ancestors before that. On her last night, several hours before she died, she remembered that she had hidden the bag a year before in the Multangular Tower on one of their rare trips into town. She was getting a bit dotty, you see, and for some reason she felt that the coins, being Roman, were sure to be safer in the ruins, protected by the gods, than tucked inside her skirt. And so she had dug a place out, between two stones, and stuck them in there, and that's why you saw Ambrose in the tower the night before her death. A wonder they had not been found by a tourist long before.

When Ambrose took the coins back to camp, the old woman gave each of the children a silver denarius and the rest to Ambrose and Rose. It was to be their birthright, you see, a remembrance of the grandmother. But Nat has no great feelings for his past or his ancestry, and your belt was too great a temptation. So he gave you his only treasure from the old woman, and Ambrose feels this to be a frightful omen for the rest of the clan.

Perhaps you can understand now why he is so anxious to have it back, and he has offered five pounds for its return. If you will mail the coin to me, I will see that he gets it, and forward a cheque to you.

Yours sincerely,
Joe

Was it something perverse in his nature, Dan wondered, or did it go deeper than that? An instinct for self-preservation, maybe? Whatever, he knew almost as soon as he had read the letter that he would not return the coin—not yet.

In the past few days he had not thought much about it, and so he had not feared it. Down here with Blossom, he was sleeping and eating well and feeling stronger than he had felt in months. To have the coin in his possession gave him a strange feeling of power, and he did not like the thought of the gypsies possessing his belt, while he in turn had nothing of theirs.

He decided to stall:

Dear Joe:

I'm staying at my grandmother's in the country for a while, and Mom forwarded your letter. You're right; it was Nat's idea that we trade, and of course I didn't know anything about the history of the silver denarius. I would much rather have my belt returned than the five pounds, however. Would Ambrose agree to that?

Sincerely,
Dan

He checked the postmark on Joe's letter. It had taken several weeks to get to him, even by air. It would take that long, then, for his letter to reach Joe, then for Joe to reach Ambrose, and finally for an answer. Six weeks, perhaps, for him to sort things through.

He left the letter in the mail basket inside the front door. Later, when Lonnie picked up the outgoing letters, Dan saw him pause before he got in the car, stare hard at the envelope, and finally, putting it back in the pile of other letters to be mailed, climb in the old station wagon and head for town.

Bee was sitting on the back steps shelling peas when Dan passed by the door toward the garden again. He wondered if she had heard about his father, or if Mother had intended for him to tell her. He put his hoe against the house, sat down beside her, and reached for a handful of pods.

"Here, now, Dan. I can do this much myself," she said determinedly.

"It's okay. I need a break." They worked for a few minutes with only the sound of peas hitting the metal pan to break the quiet.

"I got a letter from Mom, Bee. I guess Dad's going into the hospital next week for some tests. She says not to get alarmed—it's no emergency."

The gnarled fingers of the old woman paused over the pan in her wide lap and her face was drawn, the wrinkles etched even deeper. She waited.

"He hasn't been sleeping well, that's all—sort of nervous. . . ." Had they ever told Blossom about Huntington's disease? Dan wondered. Did she understand that it had happened to her own husband?

"What do they think is the matter?" she asked finally.

"We're not sure. There's a possibility, I suppose, that it's Huntington's disease." Dan watched her and saw that she knew, for her hands slipped off the edge of the pan and into her lap. She leaned back against the doorframe, staring out over the south pasture.

"It's like a streak of evil running through the family," she said at last.

"It's a hereditary illness, Bee. Evil's got nothing to do with it."

"Like a warped seed that passes from one generation to the next," she went on, ignoring him.

"Bee, you can't believe that."

"I didn't say *Brian* was evil, Dan. I said there was an evilness loose upon the family." She put the pan on the ground and leaned forward, arms resting on her knees. "It happens. Don't you doubt for a minute that it happens. Somewhere in the past, something crept into this family— an awful thing. Who let it in, or why it came, I don't know. But it passes down from one generation to the next as easily as a family heirloom. When I think how my Thomas had the disease, and I didn't even know what it was. . . .

Didn't know that my brother-in-law had it either. Thought that one had been drinking and the other was crazy, that's how much I knew about it. 'A bad lot I've got myself in with,' I used to say during the later years. And then my niece called me last February and asked me questions and told me about the sickness. And finally it all came to me—all began to make sense—the stories I'd heard about Thomas's father and his father's mother. And so I says to myself, 'Sara Blossom, you've got yourself in with one of *those* families, now, and it's somebody's got to break the chain, that's all.' I kept hoping it would be our Brian to break it. But now. . . ."

"It's nothing he can help, Bee. Scientists are studying it, and they haven't come up with an answer yet. It's not as though no one's trying."

"Don't talk to me about trying, Dan. All the sickness and suffering about, and what does the government use the money for? To build more missiles, make more bombs, send a bunch of grown men, who ought to know better, cavorting about on the moon. Streak of madness in us *all*, that's what *I* say."

Dan smiled and put one arm around her, trying to brighten her mood. "You ever run for president, Bee, you'll sure get my vote."

But it didn't help.

"Yes," she said, as if to herself. "I'd like to hear what my great-grandfather would have said about it all. I'd just like to know what the gypsy would say."

"The tinker?"

She nodded. "*He'd* know why the evil came upon us."

"The disease was on your husband's side of the family, not yours."

"Just the same, the tinker would know," Bee said, as though that answered it, and she picked up the pan and began snapping pea pods again. "It sounds like foolishness, Dan, doesn't it? But they used to say about the gypsy that he knew things with his heart that a dozen men together couldn't figure out with their heads."

"No, that doesn't sound foolish at all," Dan told her. "You may be surprised at the things I've heard and seen that I can't explain logically."

"Would I, now?" Bee said, and she studied him for a moment. "Well, it happens. Especially of late."

There was rain and wind on Friday. The sky was dark when Dan awoke and darker still by ten o'clock. At noon the clouds broke only briefly, and by two, great gusts were rattling the shutters on the upstairs windows. Dan went out to the barn to be sure the horse was in.

The cow rolled its huge brown eye at him and went on munching as Dan passed her stall. The dark interior smelled of grass and manure and mud. Dan made his way to the far door where the horse was standing, half in, half out, its coat glistening, its flanks and hoofs muddy.

"Dummy," Dan said, stroking its nose. "Don't know enough to come in out of the rain, do you?" He reached out and pulled the big barn door closed behind the animal, nudging the horse on into its stall where it stomped a bit in protest.

It was then that Dan was conscious of a slight movement up in the haymow and, turning quickly, saw a lone figure sitting on one of the bales, smoking a pipe.

"What are you doing in here?" Dan asked, and realized, even as he said it, that the answer was obvious.

Lonnie sucked again on the pipe, then removed it from his mouth. "It's the grandmother," he said, gesturing toward the house. "She don't like me to smoke in there, you know."

"She'd like it even less if she knew you were smoking out here. You could set the whole place on fire in a minute."

"I'm careful."

"Just the same. . . ." It irritated Dan the way Lonnie just sat there—no apologies, no acquiescence.

He took an old blanket from the wall and began rubbing down the horse. Out of the corner of his eye, he could see the slight movements of Lonnie's head as he inhaled and exhaled, sometimes taking the pipe out of his mouth altogether and holding it in his hand.

"Bee doesn't like the horse to get wet," Dan went on. "He should have been in before this. Sometimes the door blows shut in a storm and he can't get inside. It's best to check."

"Door was open," Lonnie said. "He just stood out there making up his mind. I figured the rain felt good on 'im after all this heat."

"Well, next time you better see that he comes on in," Dan snapped. Lonnie made no answer, so Dan finished the rubdown and hung the blanket up again.

"Bee expect you to stay around when it rains?" he asked finally.

Lonnie nodded. "There's work inside, she says. Shutters need a good nailing down, and chimney needs mortaring in the attic. I mow the fields when the sky's clear, and work in the house when it's raining."

"Better got on with it then, hadn't you?" Dan threw a few ears of corn in the cow's feed bin and went back out to the house. He was surprised at himself—at the condescending way he had spoken to Lonnie, the tone of authority, the sarcasm. Bee would not have been pleased.

He still could not understand why he resented Lonnie so. Was it because Lonnie had taken the place of a gentle neighbor? Was it anger that, when the neighbor had died, Blossom had been foolish enough to hire a man she hardly knew? Or was it Lonnie's startling resemblance to Jasper Faw? Now that Dan was back in the states and on his own turf, was he trying to show some unseen foe that he was boss?

After a while he could hear Lonnie's voice below in the kitchen with Bee, then his footsteps on the stairs, and the sound of his hammering on the shutters in the room next door.

For the rest of the day, Dan seemed to be bumping into him continually—in the hallway, on the stairs, at the bottom of the ladder to the attic. At first he felt embarrassed by what he had said earlier and was on the verge of apologizing, but by four o'clock, the resentment had built up again. It irked him that Lonnie seemed to have taken over around the house in the short time he had been here, that he advised Bee about what needed to be done, that he organized his time indifferently, and that his speech was direct and sure, without any hint of deference.

The rain now had stopped, and the sun contented itself by lighting only the edges of the clouds in the western sky, rimming them with silver against a purple velvet backdrop. The air had a strange warmth to it, and a heavy mist, almost like steam, rose from the drenched ground.

Dan watched from the hallway as Bee paid Lonnie his wages. He watched the man leave from the back door, and when Lonnie was halfway across the south pasture, Dan slipped out and followed, putting the walnut grove between them.

He felt no scruples about what he was doing. If Lonnie was going to be prowling about the house in bad weather, wandering through the upstairs rooms, they should at least know something about him, at least know where he lived. Bee relied on her hunches, and however well they might have served her in the past, she was getting too old now to manage things as she used to.

The walnut grove was just thick enough to hide him from view, but sparse enough in places that he could keep track of the lone figure who was tramping now through the tall grass beyond, heading for the woods.

Dan couldn't understand where the man was going. Lonnie could have taken the road if he lived either east or west. If he was staying north of Blossom's house, there was a narrow lane that led up beside the church, and if he lived south, he would have climbed the fence at the back of the pasture and taken the footpath in the direction of the junction. Instead, Lonnie headed for the place where Blossom's stream joined Little Donegal Creek, and the underbrush grew thick and wild.

Dan had to hurry to keep up. The gloom of the sky made it difficult to keep Lonnie in sight when he fell in the shadow of the trees. For a moment Dan thought he had lost him, then caught another glimpse and quickened his pace.

Once Lonnie stopped, his back frozen, head alert, listening. For a full minute he stood there. He did not turn around, but seemed to be sniffing the air, like an animal tracking a scent. Finally he went on, and this time Dan waited until he had rounded the bend in the path and started down the steep bank to the stream before he followed. He heard a splash, and imagined that Lonnie was wading across.

When Dan reached the bend in the path, however, and looked down, there was no sign of the young man at all—only the strange warm mist that seemed to ooze up out of the ground, covering the woods with fog.

In the days to come, Dan was acutely conscious of Lonnie's presence in and about the house. He did not always see him, but could tell by the faint trace of tobacco smoke, by small sounds or sudden silences, even, that the man was there. And then one morning, when he found Lonnie in his room, Dan had a sudden revelation: Lonnie was after the coin.

"What do you want?"

Lonnie slowly rubbed one ear. "Checking all the shutters, like the grandmother said."

"I thought you did that Friday."

"I didn't get in here."

"Mine are okay. I checked them myself."

"Well, then. . . ."

Lonnie ambled on out into the hall again.

"Look," Dan said, "I don't think you ought to just walk in and out like this. Let me know when you need to get in here."

Lonnie stood looking at him a long time. The dark eyes seemed to recede even further into the head, beneath the heavy brows. Was it only his imagination, Dan wondered, or did the thin mustache curl in contempt, following the line of the lip? Lonnie started to move on, then stopped.

"Well, then . . . ," he said once more. "Perhaps you ought to say something to me before you go tryin' to follow me home. . . ."

Dan stood riveted to the floor, his heart pounding, his eyes on the hired man. This time there was definitely a curl of Lonnie's lip, a narrowing of the eyes, as though a laugh was imminent. But there was no sound, either from the man's throat or from his footsteps, and he moved noiselessly on downstairs.

Dan knew he could no longer leave the Roman denarius in his room. He would have to carry it about with him always.

He had not actually touched it since the day he had left York when—holding the coin in his hand and staring at Micklegate Bar for the last time—the huge gateway to the city had seemed to be a living thing, a face with a huge gaping mouth and cruciform slits for eyes. A fear had raced through his chest then, making his very bones feel hollow. He had thrust the coin deep into a pocket of his wallet and had not looked at it since.

When he was sure that Lonnie was downstairs, Dan went to his bureau and took out his wallet. Holding it above the bed, he spread open the small compartment, and the silver denarius fell onto the spread.

The portrait of the Emperor Vespasian lay there before him—the large ear, the thick neck, the inscription about the edge. . . . Before he could dwell on it or recall the fear he had felt previously, Dan reached out and touched the coin—gingerly at first—and then he picked it up and set it in the palm of his hand.

Again the coin felt icy, again there seemed to be images floating across his walls, the distant sound of marching, of soldiers' rustlings and footsteps. . . . But this time Dan stood his ground, his heart racing, his temples throbbing.

"Come on!" he said loudly. "I'm not afraid."

And he was not. He was more terrified, he discovered, of having shadows lurking about, waiting in the wings, than of facing the soldiers head on and ending the suspense.

The shadows did not come any closer, nor did the sound of footsteps grow louder. When he dared them to show themselves, it seemed, they kept their distance, and this made him bolder. They considered him an equal adversary. Finally, they faded away into nothingness.

He had to devise a way to keep the coin with him always, asleep or awake. Dan looked down at himself—his feet, his hands. And then he decided upon his watch. Carefully he took his pocketknife and tediously cut a slit in the thick leather band. He had to work slowly, to make sure that the slit did not go all the way through, and when it was deep enough, he picked up the silver denarius, slipped it inside, and took the watch downstairs to the kitchen where he glued the opening shut with epoxy.

He was standing there at the counter, the watchband pinched between his fingers, when Bee came in to get lunch.

"The two of you!" she said, and her voice was chiding. "Like having children about the place."

"What's the problem?"

She humphed at him. "Lonnie says you don't want him upstairs."

"That's right, Bee. I really don't think you ought to give him the run of the house. If you need something done up there, I'll do it. I thought you hired him to do the fields."

"Well, maybe I did!" she said in exasperation, "but he's not a horse, is he? No reason he has to stay outside all the time. I've a right to invite him in."

"Of course you do, but show a little caution, Bee."

"A few days ago, he says, you were after him to do the shutters."

"I was, but I changed my mind. I'd just feel more comfortable if he stayed downstairs, that's all."

She turned her back on him as she got out the tuna fish and plunked it into a bowl. Her white hair hung in wisps about her face and down the back of her neck, and her apron came up high under her arms because there was no longer any waist to anchor it. Dan buckled his watch around his left wrist, then went over and nudged her playfully with one elbow.

"Okay, I'll be sociable," he said. "I'll even talk to Lonnie during lunch."

"Won't do any good now," she grumbled. "He's got the mower out again to finish the west field. Said he'd take a sandwich and eat it there."

"See? I try to be friendly, and what do I get?"

"Oh, you!" Blossom laughed and shoved him away. "Go on with you! Why, it's like having my own two children around again—the quarreling and conniving! Dogs are easier to raise, I swear it. *Chickens*, even!"

Dan waited till Lonnie was far out in the field and Bee had gone to bed for her afternoon nap. Then he opened the door to the cellar and went down the narrow stairs. He had a hunch that Lonnie had been down there before—

been up to something, but nothing that he could imagine made sense.

There was light this time from the long, narrow opening in the foundation where the spring water ran through. The beam of daylight coming in so close to the ground made the whole place seem a prison and cast queer shadows behind the barrels next to the wall; they squatted there, covered with moss, like ancient creatures serving out their time. The air was dank and oppressive.

Suddenly Dan felt a draft, a chill, and he fought the dread that usually followed, feeling it swell inside him. He was more certain than ever that he was not alone, yet there were no sounds, no shadows, no breath upon his neck. And then he heard it:

"Dan. . . ."

It was not like the sharp, plaster-ripping call that had awakened him each morning back in Harrisburg. It was not even the call he had heard the day he arrived. This time it was far, far away . . . a man's voice . . . as though calling from the depths of a well.

"Dan. . . ."

He whirled about, his ears straining, his eyes huge.

"Dan. . . ."

He moved over closer to the spring, then got down on his hands and knees. And there, looking up at him from the water, was the face of Ambrose Faw.

3

H E KNEW, as if from some lesson innately learned, that he should not speak the gypsy's name. As he crouched almost unbreathing beside the stream, he was aware that the face in the water grew no larger, came no closer. It was as though his own silence created a barrier through which Ambrose could not come.

Nor could Dan leave, however. He was held there at the spring as surely as if some huge hand had reached up and grabbed his neck. Yet nothing rippled beneath the surface. The face remained clear, the eyes locked in a fierce stare, the gray-black beard unruffled by the current that flowed through it. And then, as Dan watched, the lips began to stretch, the eyes to crease, the jaw to widen, and a slow smile spread across the heavy face. Dan bolted backwards, threw himself bodily on the earthen floor to break the grasp of the phantom hand, then sprang to his feet and rushed headlong upstairs, where he crumpled at the top and lay still, waiting for the banging in his chest to subside.

"So you've seen him, then?"

Dan saw his grandmother's slippered feet there beside him and sat up slowly, leaning against the doorframe. She had wakened from her nap, and her hair was still askew, hanging in long, weblike wisps about her face. She moved over to a chair at the table and sat down heavily, looking at him, waiting.

"Who?" asked Dan, wanting to draw her out. His heart still pounded, pulse still thudded.

"My great-grandfather—the tinker."

Dan blinked, hesitating, watching her carefully. "What are you talking about, Bee?"

She cocked her head. "Now don't you go trying to protect me, Dan. I know what you've seen in the stream, and you had a fright, that's what. I saw it myself just last week. It's only a fancy, I told myself, but then the next day, there it was again, so clear that if I'd a dipper, I would have brought up his beard in my cup."

"How do you know it's your great-grandfather?"

"He's the first one I thought of when I saw the face— the eyebrows, the beard—it all matches what I've heard all my life about him."

Dan got up and went over to sit at the table with her,

relieved that she knew no more, yet curious about her conclusions. She was anxious to share what she had seen.

"I've been afraid it was my mind that was going," Blossom continued. "It's what they say, you know—you see things that aren't there, hear things that never were. . . ."

"There's nothing wrong with your mind, Bee. You're as sharp as you ever were. We both saw the face, and we both can't be nuts. What do you make of it?"

"I think he's come for me, that's what. I don't mean right away, perhaps. But I'm not afraid, Dan. When you get to be old, you begin to look at death as a friend."

"You think it's the face of death, then?"

"No, only of my great-grandfather. But he's come to help me get used to the idea, you see, so that when the time comes, I'll know I have company."

The idea seemed so comforting to her that Dan did not even think of telling her otherwise. The pounding in his chest had begun to quiet; there was time, now, to work it through.

Blossom was suddenly conscious of her appearance and clumsily began arranging her disheveled hair, poking the long wisps back here and there with bent fingers. There was a pink hue to her cheeks, typical of the way she awoke each afternoon, and Dan caught a glimpse of the young woman she once had been.

Then her faded blue eyes returned to his. "You see,

Dan, everything begins and ends in the water. That's what my mother used to tell me. The oceans spit us out upon the land to live our brief lives and swallow us up again when our time is over. She always said that when you dip your hand into a river, you drink a little of what you were and what you're yet to be." Blossom leaned forward and added secretively, "There's an underground passage, you see. There are all sorts of things in the water that people don't know about, but they're there."

"What passage?"

"Well, a hole, really. Job's Hole, the local folks call it, down near the mouth of the river, where it opens into the bay."

"Where does it go?"

"I've heard some folks say there's no bottom, it's so deep. Others say it's a cave or something that runs under the Chesapeake down to Baltimore. But *some* think . . . *I* think . . . that it leads to places and things we know nothing of. . . ."

Instantly Dan thought of Lonnie: *I follow the river, go wherever there's work.* He buried his face in one hand, tired from the tension. Bee watched him.

"You don't think it was the old tinker?" she said at last.

"I don't know what to think." Dan was torn between telling her nothing and telling her everything. She would understand, he was sure. She was at ease with things she could not explain. But to tell her might also involve her somehow in the drama that seemed to be unfolding here in her house, and Dan could not bring himself to do that.

"Stay here with me this summer, Dan," Blossom said. "It's one thing to be an old lady with a cow in the barn and a horse in the pasture and no one to care for them but me. But it's quite another to be an old lady with a face in her cellar."

Dan reached over and put one hand over hers. "Promise me one thing, Bee; Lonnie's not to go down there. Okay?"

There was a battle going on in her face, he could tell. Exasperation versus fear, sympathy versus superstition.

"All right," she said finally, but her voice lacked conviction.

"And you've got to *tell* him—make it very plain," Dan said.

"If you'll stay the summer, I will."

"I'll stay." Dan reached up then and squeezed her shoulder and was surprised at how little flesh there was on her bones, how thin and fragile they were. Her age suddenly seemed to have crept up on him. He felt responsible should anything happen. As soon as Lonnie moved on, he would see about hiring someone else.

"If you see the face again," Dan told her, trying to be funny, "just let it be. You don't have to say good morning or good evening or give it the time of day."

Bee laughed then, feeling better. "If I see it again," she said, "I'll set me a bowl of potato salad right down on top of it."

Dan went over to the cellar and closed the door, as though closing it would shut off the fear, and Bee fussed about the kitchen making supper.

The sun bore down like a huge hot eye, scalding the tops of the trees so that even the shade below seemed oppressive.

Dan did not lie on the grass as he usually did over the lunch break, but sat tensely, his back against the beech tree, his muscles taut—aching in their rigidity. He could sense that Lonnie, on the other side of the trunk, was feeling the same. Like animals, whenever they were close enough to cross the other's scent, they stiffened, their eyes narrowing as though ready to spring.

Blossom sat at the old picnic table finishing her lunch, her back to the young men.

"There's a magpie on the roof of the shed," she mused.

Dan put down his sandwich and stared over at the large black bird with the telltale white on its breast.

"I didn't think there were any around these parts," he said.

"I didn't either," said Bee, "but I know a magpie when I see one. My uncle used to have one in a cage when I was

47

a youngster—taught him to speak, too. Just a few words, you know."

"Where do you think this bird came from?" Dan asked.

"Could be somebody's lost a pet, I suppose. Or else it's a long, long way from home. My aunt used to have a saying about magpies; one is for bad luck, two for good, three for a wedding, four for a death, five or six are for money, I don't know which, and . . . I could never remember what seven were for. I knew it once."

"For a story that will never be told."

Lonnie's voice came low and clear from around the trunk of the tree.

Bee turned around. "You're right! I remember now. For a story that will never be told. . . ."

The coincidences now were too uncanny to be ignored. As though speaking a foreign language, Blossom and Lonnie communicated in ways that seemed to belong to them alone. It could well have been a conversation among the Faws.

Dan looked numbly out over the fields. If he squinted just a little, blotting out the sharp details of the barn and shed, the rolling hills could well be those of the Yorkshire moors—the purplish gray of the heather, the hedgerows, the narrow lanes and stone fences. It seemed only a short step in time since he had sat with the gypsies around their fire, sharing their midday meal while Jasper, sullen and silent, had sat on the opposite bank, listening.

They were coming here, he was sure of it—had followed him through some mystery of the ocean currents. They had left the moor in the rush of the Ouse River, tumbled into the Bay of Humber, and on into the North Sea. Once in the ocean, they had followed his scent, swiftly, like living spores, waterborne; they had tracked him to the Chesapeake Bay, up the mouth of the Susquehanna, and finally into Little Donegal Creek where it joined Blossom's stream. Then silently, secretly, they had entered her house. They were here, and Bee had innocently bid them welcome.

For the next week, Dan threw himself into his work, occupying every minute of his time, trying to ignore the phantoms around him, to bore them, to make them realize the senselessness of pursuit. He thought more than once of putting the coin—the Roman denarius—in an envelope and sending it back to Joe Stanton, but something within him, deeper than reason, held him back.

He avoided Lonnie altogether, and Lonnie him. They arranged their days so that they met only once at lunchtime, and then it was under the protection of Blossom's benign chatter. Dan awoke each morning as tense and as tired as he had been when he went to bed, as though sleep had been interrupted by voices and whisperings that gave him no peace. He dreamed nothing, felt nothing while he slept, yet his body ached as if he had been on a long journey; his legs were cramped and his feet sore.

Regardless, he worked hard, the sweat pouring down his face and back. He would hoe and weed and hammer and chop, one job following on the heels of another, fearful that the least respite—a mere pause, even—would bring him closer to that which he had been avoiding.

At one point he called home.

"Dan?" came his mother's voice. "You sound so far away. Is everything all right?"

"Why wouldn't it be?" Dan said in reply. "I was wondering about Dad."

"I should have called you, I guess, but there just isn't anything new. We've been waiting for the results of more tests, anything that might give us a clue, and none of it tells us much."

"They haven't found anything?"

"Nothing significant. The doctors say that the results are inconclusive. I never knew what an awful word that is until I'd lived with it awhile. There's neither a *yes* nor a *no*. It's still a *maybe*."

"And the hand trembling?"

"They'll test him on that again in a month. But there's just no point in your coming home, dear. There's nothing you can do. It's something Brian has to learn to live with, and it's hard for him right now—hard for me, too, because he's all closed up in himself."

"I wasn't thinking about coming home, actually. In fact, I promised Bee I'd stay with her for the summer. I wanted to make sure you wouldn't need me."

"I'm glad you're staying. How is she?"

"Same as ever. Feisty."

"More feeble, though. I noticed that the last time I saw her. Tell her we'll be driving down in a few weeks to visit. Incidentally, Bill called yesterday wondering if I'd heard from you. He says he's waiting for an article for the school paper."

"Tell him I haven't forgotten. I'm working on it."

In truth he was not. Dan did not allow himself any pauses in which to write, for to keep his body busy was to keep his brain numb. As long as his arms and legs were moving, his mind was focused on them. It was only during the lunch hour and in the evening, when he first fell into bed, that his senses—having been kept in check during the day—seemed to strain at the bonds that held them, to gallop over continents and oceans and settle once more upon the gypsy camp and the face of Ambrose Faw.

And then, at the beginning of the fourth week, when Dan awakened, he heard his name so clearly, the consonants so distinct, that he leaped out of bed and stood frozen in the center of the floor.

"Yes?"

In answer, his name came again, and he wheeled about

to find the magpie on his window ledge. As he watched, the bird's beak parted, the throat swelled, and the sound cackled again from the magpie, like a laugh: "Dan."

Slowly Dan moved toward the bird, a strange fury welling up inside him. So the phantoms were surrounding him, then—flaunting their success. Well, let them come; the barn, the house, the fields, the stream, the river—all were as familiar to him as his own face in the mirror. This time, perhaps, he had the advantage.

He put out his hands to grasp the mapgie, to wring its neck. There would be no raven above his door, quothing its vapid syllabic nonsense. But his hand merely touched the wing of the bird before the huge creature spread its wings and slowly sailed out over the lawn. It circled the beech tree twice and then headed into the west.

He sat by the spring in the cellar. He had planned it carefully, waiting until Friday when Lonnie usually drove Blossom into town. He had purposely risen early that morning and mixed the paint for the upstairs hallway knowing that once he had begun, Blossom would not suggest, as she sometimes did, that he instead of Lonnie drive her. The lawn mower was being taken in for sharpening, and this would require an extra stop, another delay. The moment the station wagon left the drive, he went to the cellar and waited.

52

He did not know how he knew that he should not speak the name of the gypsy when the face appeared. Perhaps it was something Orlenda had said the day of the funeral—that one must not speak the name of the dead—that it would beckon their spirit. Ambrose, it was true, was not dead, but whatever the nature of these faces, whatever the form of the creatures, these ghosts, Dan knew that to speak their names was to summon them, and in the act of summoning, they were given a certain control over his life. And so he sat quietly by the spring, where it bubbled out from a crevice in the rock, and looked down into the shallow stream where the water flowed gently toward the hole in the foundation. Light streamed through the opening and reflected there on the surface.

But the face did not appear. For an hour Dan sat by the stream, alert for any shadow that might signal the arrival of the specters, any ripple of the water, any whispered sound amid the dampness and mold. But nothing happened.

He remembered the night in the tower at York where he had slipped from his hotel room determined to find the ghostly soldiers who shadowed his walls, to shout out the name of their emperor and dare them to take on form. What he had invoked that night by his courage, however, was Ambrose Faw. And now that he waited for the gypsy, the man did not come. He went back to the upstairs hallway and took up his brush again, frustrated and silent.

Bee and Lonnie still had not returned by lunchtime, so Dan made a sandwich to eat while he worked. The hour in the cellar had cost him some time. The upstairs was warm in the heat of the July noon, and the smell of paint made him giddy. He opened all the windows wide, hoping to flush the fumes from the bedrooms.

And then, while he was painting the space above his doorway, he heard his name. This time it had a different sound, however—a softness—and for a moment he thought that Blossom had returned. When he stepped down off the ladder, he saw the magpie sitting on the sill of his window, facing inward. Again the beak opened, again the throat swelled, and again the name "Dan" came from the bird as distinctly as if a human voice had cried it out.

Slowly Dan reached up to the top of the ladder for his half-eaten sandwich. Moving cautiously, he stooped at the door of his room and breaking off a crust, crumbled and scattered it around on the floor.

His gesture did not seem to frighten the magpie. It turned its head sideways, looking slyly at Dan with its round dark eye, and took a step or two on the ledge.

Again Dan tore a piece of crust from the sandwich and scattered it, sending it slightly closer to the sill. Again the bird turned its head sideways and watched. Then, suddenly, the magpie hopped down onto the floor, paused a moment, and began pecking at the bread.

Dan lunged. His movement was so swift, so sudden, that he hardly planned it. He sprawled there among the crumbs, arms outstretched, jaw set, and as the bird spread its wings and started to rise toward the window, Dan clasped one of its legs and held fast.

A loud screeching filled the air, and the huge bird beat its wings, sending black feathers flying. It contorted its body as it bent its head, pecking furiously at Dan's arm. Still Dan held on, stumbling to his feet, and—after retrieving a shoelace from his dresser—tied the bird's legs together. Then he grabbed the pillow on his bed with one hand, pulled off the case, and, after a fierce struggle, thrust the magpie inside.

For another minute the bird squawked and beat at the case with its wings, but when Dan twisted the opening shut and tied it with a second lace, the bird suddenly quieted and lay still.

The room was a shambles. The chair was overturned, the rug was askew, and there were feathers and crumbs scattered in all directions. Now that he had taken the magpie prisoner, Dan realized he had no idea why he had done so or what he would do with it. Hearing the return of the station wagon, he carried the pillowcase to the cellar and laid it behind the old nail kegs along one wall. He had scarcely time to run back upstairs and sweep up the feathers and crumbs before he heard Bee on the floor below.

They sat together at dinner, Dan picking at his food, Bee watching.

"I would have thought the work would make you hungry," she said finally.

"It's the heat," Dan said, pushing his plate away.

Blossom's faded blue eyes seemed brighter somehow in the evening light. She folded her fingers together at the edge of the table and then pressed forward, watching him closely.

"You and Lonnie didn't have words this morning, did you?"

Dan looked at her. "No. I didn't even talk to him. Why?"

"You acting the way you do, Lonnie acting the way he does. . . ."

"What's wrong with Lonnie?"

"I don't know, but this morning, standing there at the mower shop, he suddenly seemed so strange."

"How?"

"Just began pacing back and forth so restless-like, his face all tense, breathing short, as if he was in pain. I asked if he was all right, and he didn't answer, like he never heard me. But soon it passed, and then he was as if it had never happened. I thought maybe he was given to fits or something."

Dan thought instantly of the bird in the pillowcase. "About what time was this, Bee?"

"Oh, noon, I suppose. Maybe it was his stomach. Lonnie's used to regular meals at my place, and a man can't go very long on an empty stomach without getting dizzy."

"Probably so," said Dan, and got up to sit alone on the porch.

He waited that night until Bee had gone to bed, then sat on the bottom step outside her door, waiting still. When the silence in the house was complete, however, and he was sure she was asleep, he picked up the lantern from the wall in the kitchen, opened the cellar door, and moved cautiously down the steps into the shadows below.

Lonnie would come for the magpie, he felt sure. He was certain that there was a connection between the two and that Lonnie's appearance here on the farm had been followed by the bird's.

The trickling of water seemed all the louder because of the silence in the rest of the house. The daytime sounds from outside had also ceased—the clucking of the chickens, the buzz of locusts. There was nothing now but the bubbling of the current as it passed over the rocky bottom of the shallow stream, and with each step Dan took, the dank coolness of the cellar enveloped him more.

He paused halfway on the stairs to look around, to make sure that Lonnie had not already come and was waiting for him. He held the lantern high so that he could see behind the preserves in the pantry room and between the boxes and trunks along one wall. Finally, satisfied that he was alone, he went down the rest of the way and over to the pillowcase behind the nail kegs.

The case itself was shredded in several places, and there were claw markings on the earth beneath. Dan reached down and placed his hand on the pillowcase. The bird stirred momentarily, and Dan could feel the rapid beating of its heart beneath his palm. He felt a sudden sympathy for it and quickly took his hand away. It seemed strange that anyone or anything should fear him.

The air seemed heavy with events about to happen. It was as though, since capturing the bird, Dan's mind had opened to a new dimension, as though there were a symbiotic bond between him and the magpie and Lonnie. He sat down on a nail keg and leaned against the wall.

The night grew older, however, and still Lonnie did not come. Perhaps what Dan had thought was a sixth sense was only nonsense, an overactive imagination. Perhaps the magpie was a mere bird with a meaningless cry that Dan, in his panic, had mistaken for the calling of his name—

someone's lost pet, as Bee had suggested. He looked at his watch and thought about sleep.

And then, from somewhere, he heard singing. He tensed, ears prickling with the intensity of listening. He could make out every syllable, but understood none of it. It was the language he had heard that day in the woods near the gypsy camp—the Celtic chant, or prayer, or song—whatever. What Nat had pretended not to hear.

Fear, his old familiar friend, rose up again, pounding at the inside of his chest. It was the dread he had felt in York—the paralyzing anxiety that crippled him and left him limp.

He was terrified, but not yet helpless. He had come here to wait for a phantom, and the phantom was here. His body craved a command, a motive—anything that would propel his arms and legs and release the terror that had settled in his joints. Without knowing quite why, he wheeled about on the keg, picked up the pillowcase, and—untying the string—grabbed the magpie by its legs and pulled it out.

To his surprise, the bird did not struggle, nor even turn to peck his hand. It lay passively on its side as though dead, yet the dark eye was open, watching his every move.

Dan untied the second lace from around the bird's legs and held the magpie up high in the air.

"Come on, then," he said to the singer, and his voice

trembled with a terrible anticipation. "If you want your bird, take it."

But there were no ripples in the stream, no shadows on the wall, only a sudden chill, a cold, clammy presence of something there in the cellar beside him.

And then the breast of the bird thrust forward, the throat began to swell, and when the yellow beak opened, the Celtic words came tumbling out, sharp and clear.

In terror, Dan let go, and with a huge sweep of its great wings, the magpie flew slowly about the cellar in wide arcs, each time dipping closer and closer to the spring. On the sixth circling, it suddenly gave a cry, like that of a young girl and, as Dan stared aghast, swooped rapidly toward the crevice in the rock, from which the spring began, and disappeared.

For several minutes Dan could not move. For a brief time his fear of the bird and the singing gave way to near certainty that he was physically ill—that the fragile lining of his chest would no longer hold a heart so swollen out of proportion, so fierce in its beating that his temples pounded violently. But finally, as the silence in the cellar settled in, his pulse slowed, and he was relieved to discover that the dread itself had passed, leaving only astonishment and disbelief.

Cautiously he moved forward on his hands and knees toward the spring, certain that he would see the magpie floating dead in the water, its delicate skull caved in from the rock against which it had bashed itself. As he neared the stream, however, and peered down into the crevice, he saw not the bird, but the face of Orlenda.

4

H E DID NOT KNOW how he got outside—only that he was drenched, as though he had fallen head-first into a river. He almost remembered the falling itself—leaning forward, tipping, then down, down, sucked in by a current more powerful than he had ever dreamed, through tunnels of rock and tunnels of time, through light and dark and birth and death and oceans and oceans around him. As though he had aged and been re-born, again and again, but here he was, outside the house, trembling with cold.

There was something very strange about the house, however. It seemed to have taken on a new form, to have shrunk, perhaps, and he stared at it through the water streaming down from his hair. The landscape was Blossom's, yet not hers at all. He wondered if he had walked, dazed and disoriented, onto a neighboring farm instead.

Half-wild pigs, lean and bristled, rooted about in the underbrush.

And then he noticed his clothes. He wiped the water from his eyes and lifted one foot incredulously. There was a piece of leather for a sole, held to his foot with strips of cloth, which were bound about his leg to the knee. He wore a long shirt and a kiltlike garment over it. The coarseness of the cloth, the unevenness of the stitching, the color of the dye told him that his garments were hand-made, but so strange in their appearance he could not fathom where he had got them. Slowly he turned again, squinting in all directions, until finally he was facing the house once more.

The door opened only a crack, letting a thin beam of light sift through—a flickering beam, like that from a hearth—and then the door opened wider and someone with a shawl about her shoulders came hurriedly across the yard.

"Blossom?" Dan said, but the word sounded strange.

The moonlight fell on the face above the shawl, and Dan saw that it was Orlenda.

"Well, come in quickly then and dry yourself," she told him. "All manner of folk are about tonight, and the Romans not far off."

Dan stared at her, stunned. It was certainly Orlenda's voice—the tone, the inflection—and though she spoke in a different tongue entirely, he knew what she was saying. The words had a sound more akin to the ones he had heard near the gypsy camp or that the magpie had chanted in the cellar through its yellow beak. It was as though his ears picked up the sentences as they came from her mouth, but his brain translated them into meaning. Such things had happened in his dreams before—bizarre things that seemed to need no explanation. He had accepted them as natural and awakened to laugh about them later.

But he could not accept this, and he knew that he was not asleep. He dug his toes into the pieces of hide beneath his feet, clenched his fingers until the nails cut into the palms of his hands. He pressed his tongue hard against the back of his teeth, flexing his jaw, his neck, his shoulders, his back—tightening, testing every part of his body, inch by inch, to assure himself that he was indeed here in body as well as mind.

"Come *on*!" the girl said impatiently, pulling at his arm.

He was conscious now of the cold, of the fact that his feet were painfully chilled. The dampness of his clothes invaded his skin. He clasped himself tightly about the ribs to stop the shaking, to see if there was substance to himself. He walked, he breathed, he felt, he saw—his own body, surely—and yet he knew with a strange kind of certainty that his body still lay on the floor in the cellar of Blossom's house. He was there and he was here, returned

64

to a place and a time where he also belonged. Orlenda seemed to know him, and she was so sure of herself that he followed her willingly into the house and over to the fire in the hearth.

The mother was turning a piece of meat—a rabbit, perhaps—on a spit above the flames and turned to look at Dan.

"It's a sorry sight you are!" she cried, making way for him at the fire, a disgruntled look on her face, as though whatever had happened he had brought upon himself. "Chased by the soldiers, were you?"

"I think he's had a fall, Mother. He's not himself," Orlenda said.

"Not right in the head, eh?" The woman looked at him closely, then said to Orlenda, "Are there any left, Orlenda, who are right in the head? They leave home to join the legion, and all end up fighting each other." She grunted and spun the rabbit around once more, her eyes glowering like coals.

Dan recognized her at once as Ambrose's wife, the Rose of the gypsy camp. But it was not the gentle woman he had known on the moor; this one was tough, strong, and the furrow between her brows seemed to have become permanent. Like Lonnie, both she and Orlenda seemed older than the Faws he had known in York. It was as though he were looking into their future, and yet they were all obviously living in an age long passed. Rose, too, spoke in the same Celtic tongue as her daughter, but when she addressed her, it sounded more like "Morna" than "Orlenda." Still, Dan's mind translated for him, and he understood.

"Daniel wasn't fighting, Mother. The last patrol burned his hut, don't you remember? And then, when the Picts came and the fighting began—"

"Ah, what's it matter?" Rose shrugged it off with a wave of her hand. "And when did we last see your father, eh? Like as not it was he leading the Picts' attack." She gave a short, sharp laugh. "'The Last of the Brigantes,' the man calls himself. Ambrose has the brain of a flea, Orlenda. A common flea."

Dan tried to sort out their words. "Daniel," Orlenda had called him. At least, it came translated that way. His ears told him she had called him something else— "Duncan," perhaps. Orlenda turned and observed him curiously.

"The fighting at your hut took place many weeks ago. Where have you been all this time?"

"I don't know," Dan said, and instantly stopped, aghast at the strange jumble of words that came from his own mouth. They would think him an idiot, and there could be no other explanation than that he was going mad. He tried to stop the incessant chatter of his teeth. His chest began to ache with the cold, and even the warmth of the fire could not penetrate it.

Orlenda and Rose seemed to understand quite well, however.

"From the look of him, he's been living in the bogs. A good case of fever, that's what he's caught," said Rose, but her voice was a bit softer. She shook her head and slowly began turning the spit again, checking the meat, which dripped golden juices into the fire. "All of us—the ragged remains of the northern tribes—all together, they said, could oust the Romans once and for all and have the country to ourselves again. And meanwhile our young men make friends with the legionaries and go off to fight for the emperor. And so we have Celts against Celts. In the dark, it's brother against brother. And there is always dark here now. Everyone has become blinded by the warring."

It seemed to Dan an especially knowledgeable speech for a mere peasant. What did she know of tribes other than her own? What did she know of a Roman emperor? Like the Rose of the gypsy tribe, she seemed to have a special gift for looking backwards, for seeing the present as though it were past and announcing the judgment that was yet to come.

He did not care to get into a discussion with the woman, however. He did not even wish right now to sort things through. He ached with the cold, and the heat of the fire only made his raw hands sting.

"Sit on the hearth," Orlenda told him, and helped unwind his foot wrappings. "Why didn't you come here at once? You knew we would feed you, give you bed . . ." And when he didn't answer, she put one hand lightly on his brow. "It's cool, Mother," she said, relieved. "Maybe he'll escape the fever after all."

Dan curled up on the stones, his back to the fire, and let the shivering overtake him. Orlenda covered him with a rough blanket and thrust a pillow of straw under his cheek. "Sleep, then," she said, and sat down beside him, while her mother, at the other end of the hearth, continued turning the spit. Dan drifted off to the sound of fat hissing and sputtering as it hit the flames.

He did not know how long he slept, but when he awoke he tried to orient himself before opening his eyes, tried to guess where he lay and what he was wearing. The coarseness of the blanket told him, and when he opened his eyes again, he was reconciled to the room as it was before, to Orlenda's soft breathing somewhere beyond his head.

There were open beams across the ceiling, just like the ceiling in Blossom's kitchen, but beyond the beams, he could see the thatch of the roof. Then he saw Rose sitting at the table, holding a piece of the cooked meat in her hand. She tore off pieces now and then and handed them to a small girl who sat at the other end.

Slowly he sat up, conscious of the tremendous heat of the fire behind him. The back of his shirt felt as though it were scorched, and he brushed it quickly with his hand to make sure he was not threadbare.

Both Orlenda and her mother broke into loud laughter at the sight.

"Scorched the tail on you, did it?" Rose said, and motioned toward the table. "Come sit and have supper with us, Daniel. Move over there, Rachel, and let him share the bench."

The small girl scooted silently to one side.

Orlenda got up from the hearth and poured something hot and strong into a mug for him. Dan went groggily to the table in clothes that had dried stiff. He stepped over the bench and sat down by Rachel, smiling at her slightly as he did so. He wondered if she remembered him from the gypsy camp. She had grown several years older since then, but still stared as a small child stares at a stranger.

It occurred to him suddenly that there were no men about at all, and he looked around the room. No cloaks, no weapons, no pipes, no foot gear. . . .

"Where's Nat?" he asked Orlenda. The strange words slipped from his lips as though he had been raised on the language.

The girl and her mother exchanged glances, but more,

he thought, from what he had said than the way he had said it.

"It's you should know," Rose said, and again there was an edge to her voice. "It was you who talked of the glories of Londinium—of the Roman villas of the south, of the fortresses and splendors. If it hadn't been for your tales, he never would have been so eager to follow the legionaries back to Eboracum. By now, I suppose, he's a helmet on his head, and like as not, he'll fight his father, should they ever meet."

Dan put his face in his hands and leaned his elbows wearily on the table. "I'm sorry. I don't remember at all." And in truth he did not. He had obviously lived here before, but what kind of a person had he been? What had he done? Was he a friend of Rome? Perhaps. But a friend of Orlenda's as well.

Orlenda came over and pushed the bowl of rabbit meat closer to him, urging him to eat. "Daniel," she said, "you've had a fall, and your memory is rattled. Don't mind Mother. It wasn't all your fault that Nat joined the legion. His friends were doing it too—protecting the empire from the pirates, that's what the soldiers said they were doing."

"And who's to protect us from the protectors?" Rose mused as if to herself. She held her steaming mug in both hands, letting the mist warm her face. The vapor seemed to soften the lines. "Babes, yet," she said gently. "Soldiers marching, metal flashing, and off the children go to join up. And what a sorry sight the legion is now. It wasn't always so. My grandfather talked of the Roman battles he had heard of as a child—soldiers marching abreast, shields held out like a wall in front of them, heads up, going into battle row by row, the second row stepping over the bodies of the men in front as they fell, and the third row stepping over them. They would fight to the death, and the centurions with them—a sight to see, when the Red Crests went to battle. Now they straggle along in kilts half ragged, sandals flapping, in need of repair. Rome has all but forgotten them, and why they stay, I don't know. What is there now that would capture a young lad's fancy, I ask you? A legion is desperate when it puts a helmet on a young boy like Nat."

She turned to Dan. "But war is war, whether the army is splendid or desperate. It is madness no matter who wins. No, Daniel, Orlenda is right, it wasn't your fault. Even before your stories, Nat wanted to leave us. Adventure, excitement. . . . He wasn't the first who heard about the wonderful land to the south and thought perhaps the legion would put him there. You've been a good neighbor to us these last few months since the men went off. Tell me, have you been to Eboracum? Have you seen Nat since he left?"

Dan's head whirled in confusion. A neighbor, they

called him. A teller of tales. What did he know about the glories of old London and York—Londinium and Ebora-cum, as they were known here—except for what he knew back in Harrisburg, in another time? How could he have told Nat of things he had since read only in travel guides and history books? Was it possible that before living here in this place, he had lived in the future? Was he going backwards or forwards? Orlenda and her mother and sister were older than when he had known them in a future that was yet to be. His mind reeled with the weight of it and he shook his head.

"Where are Jasper and Ambrose, then?" he asked numbly.

All three at the table stared at him.

"Daniel, truly your mind has been affected. All these months you have been helping us here because the men have gone, and still you don't remember?"

"No," said Dan feebly, "I don't remember."

"It's all right." Orlenda was patient. "Jasper. . . ." She paused. "Jasper was never right in the head, you see. . . ." She waited, but Dan said nothing. "He has never really lived here with us, but prefers the woods and the birds, and he comes and goes like an animal. We put food out for him, of course; and when he's ill, he comes sometimes and lies on the doorstep, but after we tend to him and he's bet-ter, he goes back to the marshes. 'The Mad Man,' some of the tribespeople call him. Others call him 'The Bog Boy,' and the stories they weave about him are quite miraculous—that he can live underwater for weeks, neither eating nor breathing. It's all nonsense, of course. As for my father, he has the idea that it will be he who conquers the legion at Eboracum. Not in a grand battle. Not that way. He and the other tribesmen would be no match for the army. Instead they ambush the patrols that are sent out from time to time. Every time a patrol comes through, there's a battle, and men are killed on both sides. We've noticed that the patrols come by less and less, and someday they will be afraid to come up here at all. Then Father will lead the tribesmen to the very walls of the city. That is his dream, to conquer Eboracum. But it will end unhappily for us, no matter which way. For if the fort falls, Nat will fall with it. And if Rome should send reinforcements to Eboracum and make a great campaign against the tribesmen, we will lose my father and possibly our own lives as well." She sat with her chin resting in her hands on the table, and then, as if to herself, she said, "It is the worst possible time to be alive, and the worst place to be. I have thought so many times."

Dan would have liked to reply, to have said something comforting, but he could not. Tiredness overcame him again, and he discovered he was much too tired to eat. He got up and went back to the hearth, sitting this time with his back against the adjoining wall. He felt his head sinking down upon his chest, and he raised it quickly, conscious of his lack of sociability. But again the heaviness of his eyelids proved too much for him, and when he felt his head bobbing once more on his chest, he let it be. He had come a long way this night, but not half as far, he sensed, as he had yet to go.

He remembered being moved, sometime during the night, to a pallet of straw in one corner of the cooking room. He remembered the sight of his kilt drying there by the hearth and of the young child, Rachel, looking at him from the doorway of the next room. But then he gave himself over to sleep, wholly and completely, and when he awoke at last, refreshed, he thought perhaps he had dreamed it all. But the hut remained and his back itched from the straw beneath.

What was he to make of it, then? And what was expected of him? Or was he here in this time and place for no reason other than that it had simply happened, a mere whim of the universe? He thought suddenly of his father, and wondered about him. What had predestined Brian Roberts to be born into a family with Huntington's disease, and Dan along with it? What determined some to be born before the advent of penicillin and others to be born after? What mad god would protect a boy until he reached his manhood and then allow him to march off to battle? Had there ever been a time of reason, of justice—a golden age in which to be alive? Or was it always too late for one thing and too soon for something else?

His head reeled with ideas that crowded one upon another. Which was his true time on the planet—now, or back in Mt. Joy with Blossom? Was it possible that once, almost sixteen hundred years ago, he had lived here, among these people?

There were stirrings in the next room. Dan hastily got up from the straw and pulled on his stiffly dried kilt, shaking his head to clear it of sleep.

Orlenda pushed aside the doeskin that covered the doorway and came into the cooking room. She smiled when she saw that he was up.

"You're feeling better, then," she said, looking him over. "But you ate nothing last night."

He smiled. "I won't disappoint you this morning."

"Good. When I get the kindling for the fire, I'll make something hot," she said, and Dan went along to help.

A great mist seemed to rise from the earth, as though the very ground were smoldering, and the trees hung heavily with a dew that made them appear grayish-purple in the background. The moment they were out of sight of the hut, Dan was startled by the way Orlenda clutched him, her face anxious.

"Daniel, I must tell you," she said quickly, "I want to go away and beg you to help me."

He stared at her, wondering.

"Where do you want to go?"

"Mother has always talked of the land to the west, where her people are from. I want to go there. It's far away, beyond a place called Deva, near another sea. Mother says she has never seen it herself, but there the people live in peace."

"How will we find it? I remember almost nothing of the land."

She looked at him again, wary of his condition, and began talking more slowly, more patiently, as one talks to a dim-witted child. But there was no mockery in her voice.

"First we would take the road to Eboracum. I know it's dangerous, and surely we will meet the patrol along the way, but we must talk them into letting us pass."

"Would they stop a young woman who was only traveling?" Dan asked.

"They would suspect me of treachery, I'm sure, especially if they knew whose daughter I am. I want to take Rachel with me and would tell them that we have been left homeless and seek to be servants in Eboracum. There's a civil settlement there now, they say, across the river from the fort. We would work there awhile, rest, and take up food before we started off again. We would head for Deva and hope that, once there, someone could direct us to the land that Mother always talked about. But it will be diffi-cult traveling with Rachel. She's small and tires easily. It will be hard for her to keep up."

"And your mother?"

"She would never go. I've talked to her of it many times, but she won't let me speak of it now. It would be too awful for her to leave Ambrose and Jasper behind, and she lives with the hope that Nat will come back again. But I am terrified here, Daniel—not only for my sake but for Rachel's. The patrol will return. I'm sure of it, and they will be looking for the house of Ambrose Faw. When they find it, they'll not leave one of us alive."

"But surely Nat would not let them harm you."

"He may not come with them. Only some of the men go out at one time. I want to leave soon, Daniel. Tomor-row, even!"

"What do you want me to do?"

"Find the road to Eboracum. I don't even know where it is. When you do, come back for us and we'll be waiting. If we traveled together . . . well, it would perhaps appear we were husband and wife. . . ." She blushed slightly, but did not take her eyes from his face, "And you could leave me whenever you liked, once we got to the settlement. Help me get that far. If I were accepted there and worked for a time as a housemaid, I could get a pass to travel on the roads like a Roman citizen and go freely from there to Deva."

"But then there would be tribesmen to contend with."

"That I can handle. I can speak the languages of the tribes."

"Your mother will be so unhappy. . . ." Dan said, wanting to make sure she had thought of the consequences.

"I know, but she'll be glad to learn that Rachel and I are safe. There are times I suspect that she has wanted us to leave but could not bear to suggest it. This will make it easier for her. And perhaps, once we are gone, she can be persuaded to follow us."

"Then I'll go as far as you need me," Dan told her.

She leaned her head against him in relief and gratitude, and then, wordlessly, went on gathering the sticks, Dan beside her.

He knew how she felt about waiting. He could never understand how his own father could tolerate the suspense of not knowing. He did not understand how young men could wait uncomplainingly for their eighteenth year and then march off to wars they had not made, or how cities could go about their daily commerce knowing that one day—soon, perhaps—they would be under siege.

Dan wanted to scream out his anger and get it over with. He wanted to meet the enemy, whoever it was, face to face. He wanted the worst possible thing to happen so that he could deal with it and get on to other things. But life was not like that. The possibilities were always there, waiting, and he had to live both as though they were and were not.

"In a day or two, then," said Orlenda, as they went back toward the hut.

The afternoon moved in patterns of light and dark, of sun and shade, heavy with blue peat-smoke from the hearth. Dan had thought he might leave that same day to look for the road, but as soon as he had eaten, he found that his strength was uncertain. He felt like an old man, for his bones creaked and his muscles stiffened. His body, his mental processes, he knew, had been through a drastic ordeal, and he decided to give himself one more night of rest.

He was just about to drift off when he heard soft footsteps on the floor of the next room and opened his eyes. For a moment he thought that Orlenda might come to him, that for some reason she might want to leave this very night. When the doeskin curtain parted, however, it was not Orlenda who came through the opening but her mother.

The long black hair hung loosely about her shoulders, and she wore an outdoor cloak that swept the floor. Stealing softly to the hearth, she lit a torch from the burning coals and swiftly moved out through the door and into the night.

Dan got up and followed her, wondering. The suspicion at once crossed his mind that it might be Rose herself who was going about at night burning huts, not the Romans. Was it possible? Was she trying to rally the farmers, the tribespeople, against the legion?

Closing the door softly behind him so that it would not rattle in the wind, following the light of the torch that moved, bobbing and turning, on the path ahead, Dan went out into the cold. The air was dank and heavy, and he could barely see the light ahead of him, as though night vapors had dimmed it or snuffed it out.

Then he was aware that the torch had come to a stop, and he realized that he had come much further into the forest than he and Orlenda had been that morning. He was surrounded on all sides by towering oaks, and he crouched down in the brush, hugging himself with his arms for warmth. But his eyes did not leave Orlenda's mother. She stood in the center of the trees, tall and statuesque, like an oak herself, and lifted her arms to the sky. In a singsong voice, she issued a call to some unseen god, the torchlight flickering on her face.

Several times she raised her arms, and several times she issued the call—the chant rising and falling upon the silence of the woods. Then, through the brush on the other side of the clearing, illuminated by the light of the torch, came a creature half crawling, half crouching from out of the darkness. At first Dan thought it was a wolf, for there was fur on its back. Yet gaping through the mist, Dan could make out bare hands and feet and then the face—dyed a strange blue, with a thin mustache above the lip. The hair, chalked with lime, had been combed straight up, and a wolfskin had been thrown over the shoulders. Into the light of the torch the creature came, and in its hands it carried a black bird.

There was a blur of motion, a glint of metal, a shriek, a whirl of feathers, and then the bird was flapping about this way and that, making strange markings upon the dirt. Dan gasped and drew back deeper into the brush. Rose remained absolutely motionless, even when the bird flapped at her feet and spattered her cloak with its blood.

When the body lay still, Orlenda's mother knelt down and seemed to be examining the marks that the blood had made, then spoke to the strange man-creature. But the creature made no reply, and finally the woman lifted her face again and sang once more to the sky.

Dan, fearful that she might be ready to return, fled silently back along the path toward the hut. He managed to get beneath the covers before the door opened and Rose came inside. His heart thudded noisily there on the straw, and he tried breathing through his mouth to quiet it, to pretend to sleep. He heard the footsteps cross the earthen floor toward him, stop briefly beside his pallet, and then move on into the other room.

✻ ✻ ✻

"Her ancestors were Druids," Orlenda explained the next morning. Dan had followed her down to the stream for water, and when they were a safe distance from the hut, told her what he had seen. "There are times, when we are under great stress, that she performs the Druid rites—as well as she remembers them. It's a comfort to her, that's all."

"And the bird, slaughtered there in the clearing?"

"A sacrifice. She predicts the future by studying the markings of blood upon the ground. Other nights she goes to the spring, for she believes that she can contact the spirits there."

"Was the young man Jasper?"

"Yes. He's never very far away. He always knows when Mother goes into the forest. It's always Jasper who brings the sacrifice."

"He looked very strange."

"I know." Orlenda filled her clay pot with water. "He's taken on the markings of the Picts and some of the other tribesmen and paints his face with woad, but they only laugh at him and call him mad."

"Has he always been like this, Orlenda?"

"No. When I was very young, the youngest I can remember, we lived to the north, even further than Isurium. My father's people were from the highlands, and my mother's from the west, and we were only a small tribe, moving from place to place, building shelters as we went. We knew about the Romans at Eboracum, but we kept out of their way and didn't fear them much." Orlenda sat down on the bank and drew her knees up against her chest, encircling them with her arms.

"When Jasper was six, though, and I was three, we made our way during the warm season to the sea. It was a good year, Mother said, and we were able to walk in the forests with our feet unbound. We camped for a time near a fishing settlement. My father hunted in the forest and we gathered berries, and these we traded with the people in the settle-ment for their fish. Everything that was ours, we carried on our backs. It was the first time I had seen the sea, and I was so happy then, playing with the shells on the shore.

"Sometimes my father would leave us and hunt in the forest for several days or longer. It was on a morning he was gone that we woke very early to the sounds of screaming in the settlement. Mother says that she picked me up in her arms while my grandmother took Jasper's hand. We all ran to see what was wrong. I remember that part, the running. Mother said that she could not understand the commo-tion, because women were grabbing their children and running off into the trees, and men were filling their water skins with rocks. All Mother could see, looking over the cliff, was a beautiful boat with sails of skins that made loud flapping noises as the boat anchored there below. We had never seen such a boat, she said, and she thought perhaps the villagers had not seen one either. For a moment she watched the people running and tried to tell them not to go, that the noise was only the sound of the sails blowing in the wind. And then she saw the men leaping over the side of the boat and coming up the cliff with swords in their hands. It was then that she screamed too and turned to follow the others."

Here Orlenda's eyes filled with tears. They hung for just a moment on her lashes and then receded. "My grandmother did not make it. She just couldn't keep up. Mother said she turned once and saw that Granny was behind her, but when she turned again, Granny was gone, and Jasper with her."

Orlenda swallowed, gulping down the tears that rolled backwards from her eyes. "It's strange, but I don't remember anything more about that morning, only the men coming up the cliffs and my mother screaming. I do remember things about my grandmother, though. She would often tell me stories and hold me in her lap—stories about birds and rivers and trees so big you could hide in them. But that day. . . ." She sighed, and quickly wiped one arm across her eyes. "Mother continued to run. The men of the fishing village climbed trees, she told me, and showered the invaders with stones, but Mother did not stop. She cut through the forest to where the marsh grass grew, and there we hid, half under water. She said that I kept very quiet, and we stayed for several hours until the forest, with all its

84

screams and cries, had grown silent. When finally she thought it safe to come out, she went looking for my grandmother and Jasper. Perhaps it's good that I remember nothing more—I had gone to sleep on her shoulder. All about her lay the bodies of the villagers, women and children slain along with the men, their dark blood upon the sand. And there she found my grandmother, her throat slit, her body small and frail there at the edge of the forest. And hidden in a thicket was Jasper, but he was not the Jasper Mother knew. His eyes, she said, were like the eyes of a wild animal, and when she reached out for him, delirious with relief that he had been spared, he drew away from her. And he has never spoken a word from that day. All that he had seen has sealed his lips forever. He had seen my grandmother slain, for she lay only a short distance from him. The pirates had taken every bit of food from the settlement—all the fish, the berries, the animal skins, the wine. They left Jasper's body, Mother always said, but they took his soul."

"Orlenda, I'm so sorry," Dan said, putting one arm about her shoulders, and then she wept.

The tears did not last long, but when they were over, Orlenda stayed with her head against him, and Dan was glad, for he liked the warmth of her long hair, the softness of her shoulders.

"When my father came back from hunting that night

and found out what had happened, he picked up a hat that one of the pirates had worn, waded out into the sea, and flung it out over the water, uttering a Brigante oath. And then, when he saw what had happened to Jasper, he wept. It was the only time, Mother says, that she ever saw him weep, and he never cried again."

Orlenda moved one hand back and forth through the water, her thoughts far away: "My father took us deep into the forest and built us this hut. He taught us to hide in the bogs all day, if necessary, should the pirates come again. Once, when the Roman patrol came by and we were frightened, we hid in the marsh that way, and they never found us. But they will come again and again, Dan, and I'm so sick of all the fighting. Nat and Rachel were born after we settled here, so they knew nothing of the pirates. All Nat knew of the Romans, in fact, were the stories you told him about their beautiful cities in South Britain and their grand baths and the temples for their gods. When they came riding through a year ago, he was taken with their splendor—the horses, the armor, and the gleam of their helmets and swords in the sun. A sorry-looking lot they were, actually—not at all like the Romans you had told him about. But he is young and impressionable and saw only the glory. And so he followed them like a puppy, and we heard later that he had joined the legion in Eboracum. There are few Romans left, you know, in the legion; more and more they are men from the countryside. War makes enemies of friends." She shook her head. "At least he was not with them when they came through a few weeks ago and burned your hut. That much we know."

"You must have been very upset when Nat went off."

"Sad, that's the better word. But Father is furious that the legion would take a son of his. He has vowed vengeance upon the Romans, as he vowed his hatred for the pirates. One day, I'm afraid, he will be killed, and his head put on a post at the gate to the city. The patrol will come here to this hut and will kill the rest of us, too. Mother keeps praying that things will be as they once were when the family was all together. But that can never be. It's hard for her to realize that—hard for both of my parents to understand that the world has changed so much. There are no Brigantes about any more, nor Druids either. And yet they go on living as though there were. That's why I want to leave, Daniel."

"It will be dangerous. You know that."

"But more dangerous to stay."

"What do you really know about the land of your mother's people? It may be very different now from what you imagine."

"Still, I want to try," Orlenda said, and Dan knew by the set of her mouth that if he did not help her she would go alone.

"All right," he said. "I'll go this morning and search for the road. When I find it, I'll be back for you and Rachel."

They returned to the hut where Orlenda gave him a bowl of hot broth and some hunks of bread to fortify him. Rachel was playing near the fire with a doll made of rags, and Rose was dragging the bedding out of the sleeping room to air on the thicket. When her back was turned, Dan got up from the table and, with Orlenda's dark eyes upon him, slipped out the door and quickly made his way through the trees.

Ambrose, Dan decided, had chosen the spot well. Scarcely was he beyond the clearing, heading southward, when his nostrils detected the queer rooty smell of a bog. The ground beneath him became spongy, and a few feet further, he began sinking up to his ankles. He quickly withdrew and charted a new route through a dense growth of birch and hazel thickets, keeping the sun in mind. Hours later he noticed that the trees were beginning to thin out; here and there were patches of open sky. He must be coming upon a stretch of the moors; the road to Eboracum, if indeed there was one, should be close by. A road would make traveling easier, but not necessarily any more safe. It might be better to follow it from the thicket instead, traveling by night and sleeping by day.

He wondered about the land of the west that Orlenda

spoke of. Could she be referring to what would someday be Wales, or Ireland beyond? And what assurance was there that somewhere along the way they would not be set upon by fierce warriors coming down from Caledonia or, even if they found the land beyond Deva, the tribesmen of Wales? What did Orlenda really know of the world other than what she had learned from her mother? Yet she had looked so helpless, so terrified, there in the clearing. Dan longed to take her away and protect her always, always from whatever threatened her.

A twig snapped, and Dan jerked his head to the right, seeing no one. Then he thought he sensed movement in the other direction and quickly looked to the left. Nothing. He quickened his pace, but not too noticeably, not wanting to show fear, yet determined to reach the openness of the moor as soon as he could. The trees became fewer and fewer, and as he stepped out onto the moor at last, he felt the springy crunch of bracken and heather beneath his feet.

There was no road that he could see, yet it was very much like the countryside in which he had traveled about with Joe Stanton—bleak landscape, dark shadows of clouds sweeping across the barren hills. If this was his present, did the summer he had spent in York lie yet ahead of him?

There was a sudden crash in the underbrush behind him, and Dan turned to see a Roman centurion striding through. Instantly Dan whirled about and sprinted forward, driven by an animal instinct to move. There was no thought, no plan, other than to get away. Like a wild man he leaped over a rock in his path, running with back bent, as though ducking crossfire—struggling, with every ounce of effort—for the hill.

The centurion was close behind, his armor clanking as he came, and Dan remembered the soldier's spear. It would take only a single throw to hit him. The legionaries, he knew, were expert marksmen, and he a living target, silhouetted against the sky, impossible to miss. His back tingled with the awful expectancy of the javelin's tip, his ears strained for the whirring sound of a spear in midair.

But the spear did not come. Gasping and panting, Dan was tempted to turn around, to see how near the soldier was, but he could hear breathing close at his heels and dared not slow for a second. There was now nowhere on the hill to hide, no place to seek refuge, and at that moment the centurion lunged. Dan felt a strong hand on the calf of his leg. He yanked his foot free only to feel it secured by the other hand, and he fell to the ground, twisting over on his back.

Instantly the soldier was upon him, the cold metal of his breastplate pressing against Dan's chest. He had thrown down his javelin and unsheathed his dagger, but that, too, he threw beside him.

Dan's heart leaped in terror. If the soldier did not want his life, what then? His mind? His will? He cried out in panic, struggling to get a hold on his adversary, to push him off, to run again, but where, he didn't know.

The armor on the centurion's shoulders was fitted in vertical strips like the hide of an armadillo, and the curved metal bands that bound his chest were also fitted one over the other, held together in front with leather straps. Dan seized one of the straps, pushing with all his strength, and managed to shove the centurion off to one side, throwing himself on top of him.

The soldier, despite his short height, was by far the stronger and, with all his armor, heavier, too. With one muscular arm he grabbed Dan by the throat, pushing him away, gaining the advantage. Dan pummeled fiercely at his attacker, but the blows only made strange clanking noises as they struck the metal.

Somewhere off on Dan's right, a figure moved against the line of the trees, watching cautiously. Dan cried out once more in hope that someone would come to help. But the figure disappeared again into the shadows and did not return.

The dagger lay within reach. At one point Dan's hand came as close as an inch to it. One lunge and he would have it. One thrust in the back, beneath the soldier's breastplate, and the fight would be finished. As they rolled there on the ground, the metal actually touched his hand, yet Dan did not pick it up. The opportunity came and went, and yet neither of them took it.

The senselessness of the struggle began to irritate him. It was an exercise in idiocy. What grudge was there? What need of force, what show of strength? What possible use could Dan be to this man?

His limbs began to ache with weariness. The centurion, too, was tiring. Perspiration dripped from both their faces, mingling together. The air was pungent now with the odor of sweat, of damp leather, and the sharp metallic smell of armor.

The sound of the centurion's breathing had become more human, dulled by fatigue, more typical of a man grown weary of battle. He rolled over suddenly and sat up, facing Dan, his shoulders heaving with exertion, and Dan knew at that moment that he was looking into the eyes of Joe Stanton. But the centurion gave no sign of recognition.

"Be still, now," the soldier said at last. "I have need of you."

It was impossible to even consider running again. Dan bent his head, resting his arms on his knees, panting furiously, his heart knocking hard against the wall of his chest. Somehow there ought to be a way to communicate, to remind the centurion that once, in a different time, they had been friends.

"Joe?" he said finally, yet his lips said, "Justin?"

The centurion studied him hard. "Do I know you, then?" A crease appeared over the scar above the nose, as though he were troubled with a memory he could not quite recall. "You gave us meat, perhaps? Or drink?"

"I thought you'd remember," Dan said, not knowing himself.

"Of what tribespeople are you?" the centurion asked.

"No tribe," said Dan. "A farmer, only. A Briton. . . ."

"A farmer, a Briton," the centurion repeated derisively. "Every Briton up here has a tribe. Look, now." Again he grabbed Dan by the throat and this time he picked up the dagger from off the ground and held it under Dan's left ear. "As a centurion of Rome, under the Emperor Honorius of the Western Empire, I command you to do this thing I will ask."

The cold metal pressed harder against Dan's neck. He could not answer, could not even nod.

"Go to Eboracum swiftly," the centurion said. "Tell the Chief of the Legion that our patrol has been cut off. We are greatly outnumbered by a swell of tribesmen and they are sure to attack. Mark well our location and get there with all haste. We number only thirty."

The large hand released him suddenly, and the centurion reached into the pouch at his side, taking out a piece of silver.

"Take this denarius and show it to the chief. If you

reach there before nightfall, he will reward you with ten times the number. But if you fail and are found with the coin upon you, your body will be chopped into ten pieces and fed to the crows. Go now. Quickly. If you are indeed a farmer, as you claim, the tribesmen will let you pass."

The hand that held his throat now pressed the silver piece into Dan's hand and then jerked him roughly to his feet. Off to the right, Dan could see the glint of metal in the trees and knew that other soldiers were watching. But the centurion was pointing southwest, far across the stretch of moor, to another bank of trees.

"Beyond those trees," he said, "you will find the road to Eboracum. If you hurry, pausing neither to eat nor sleep, you will reach the fort before nightfall."

Dan set off at a brisk pace as the centurion retreated once more into the woods behind him. The wind penetrated his clothes, whipping at his long shirt as he crossed the moor. He did not look back. Ahead, he knew, were the tribesmen, waiting. His heart pounded against his chest.

He was glad he had come alone this first time, glad he had not subjected Orlenda and Rachel to the ordeal of seeking out the road. The gray sky had completely obliterated the sun, and the air was damp. He stumbled along the rocky ground, his neck still hurting from where the centurion had grabbed him, his mind numb from all he had seen and heard.

It was Joe Stanton, surely, but there had been only a

hint of a memory in his eyes. What was it he remembered? Dan wondered. Certainly not the night they had wrestled outside of York. That was all to come much later. And yet Dan remembered.

He thought briefly of throwing the coin away and going back an alternate way. He had promised nothing, had spoken almost nothing. But if he were caught returning, if it was discovered that he had not done as the centurion had commanded. . . .

And then he remembered Orlenda, waiting. She would bring along a cooked bird and some bread and cheese, she had said, and would put all of Rachel's clothes upon her, in readiness. They would go to bed and, when they were sure that the mother was asleep, would come out of the hut and Dan would meet them.

If he went on to Eboracum now, even running as swiftly as he could, he doubted he would reach it before dusk, and perhaps the legion would not send reinforcements until morning. If the tribesmen were going to attack, as the centurion said, it could be any time at all. The battle would be over, and Dan's mission would be futile. Still, the look in the centurion's eyes. . . .

Throw the denarius away, his senses told him, but he could not. Also, Orlenda might need it once she reached the settlement. Whose side was he on? That was the question. If he did not go for help, Joe and the other soldiers might be slaughtered. But if he did, and the whole legion marched northward, might not the soldiers take reprisals against all Britons in these parts, women and children included?

When he reached the trees, he stopped suddenly and tied the coin up in one corner of his long shirt. Then, turning about, he headed east, hiding himself in the thicket, hoping to go back a long way round and reach Orlenda by nightfall.

5

I T WAS NOT an easy journey, and it was not his feet that hurt him, or the cold, but his conscience. Thirty men were at his mercy, and he had turned his back on them. The face of Joe Stanton seemed to rise at every turn in the gray mist, slowing his steps, as though he were walking against the wind. Once he stopped, his palms wet with indecision, and turned back toward Eboracum. Then he thought of Orlenda and turned northeast once more.

His head throbbed as if with fever, and he stumbled on. It seemed increasingly clear that his mission must be to rescue Orlenda and Rachel. If there was a purpose to his being here, if there was any meaning in his life, he would find it in the service of peace, of that he was sure. There would be a battle regardless, if not now, sometime soon. The fighting would continue until the Romans left Eboracum forever and the land were returned to the Britons, or it would go on

until the rebellious tribes of the north had been so deci-
mated and ravaged that they lost the will to fight.

What was right, then, and what was wrong? Dan could
not remember what he had told Nat about Londinium and
the other Roman cities in the south. But if what Orlenda
said was true about their fine homes, their baths, their
temples, their courts, their vineyards—what an elegant
land it must be! What a contrast between the civilized
world of the Romans and the painted Picts of the north.
Why did the tribespeople protest so vigorously over the
culture coming their way, when the Romans were said to
be tolerant of the religions and social customs of the
Britons they conquered?

Yet the Romans—what was it to them that land and
still more land should be added to the empire? How many
acres were worth a man's life? To the man who gave it, was
the reward ever high enough? Who decided that a man
should fight? The men who did the fighting or the emperor
in his palace back in Rome? The thoughts tumbled swiftly
through his mind, one leaving as another came to take its
place. It helped to feel angry at both sides; he wanted none
of their wars.

Dusk was settling now over the countryside, and his
only sense of direction came from the wind, which blew
from the west. Feeling it against his left cheek, he kept his
footsteps northward.

Suddenly he froze, aware of a movement in the bushes ahead. He stood motionless in his tracks, his muscles taut, waiting, watching, his ears straining for the slightest sound. Had the soldiers been following? Had they seen him turn back? There was a rustle of underbrush behind him, and then swiftly, from all sides, the thicket gave way and he was surrounded by tribesmen. He had not thought he would run into them going back. Ambrose had planned it so that not only was there a wall of tribesmen ahead of the soldiers, cutting them off from Eboracum, but tribesmen beside and behind them as well.

What a strange assortment of men they were: there were those with the blue faces, those with saffron-colored cloaks; there were men with skins thrown over their shoulders and kilts about their loins, and magnificent men naked to the waist, their features finely chiseled, eyes of blue.

Dan was seized by rough hands and dragged in among the trees where he was thrown at the feet of a huge figure who was sitting on a tree stump, eating his evening meal. Even before Dan raised his head, even before he focused his eyes, he knew he was lying at the feet of Ambrose Faw.

The eyes were even more fierce than Dan had remembered. The heavy jowls, the gray-black mustache above the lip, the beard that flowed wild and unruly down upon the mammoth chest—a bear of a man sitting there in his saffron cloak and kilt of goatskin.

Without rising, Ambrose thrust out one foot, bound with rags and skins, and kicked Dan as one might kick a dog lying in the path.

"Ambrose," Dan said quickly, remembering that they had supposedly been neighbors once, "don't you recognize me?"

"I recognize you all too well," Ambrose answered, "and you have the look of treachery on your face. What a pity that you did not go down in ashes along with your hut."

"I remember nothing of the hut burning," Dan said quickly. "Orlenda told me that the soldiers had come."

"You remember nothing? Nothing?" Ambrose mocked him. "You do not remember how the centurion knocked on your door and instead of greeting him with a bucket of scalding water you let him enter? You let his men sit at your table. You allowed them to ravish your cupboard and refresh themselves. Why didn't you wash their feet for them, Daniel? Why didn't you draw their water, sing them songs, and offer them your bed as well? There are those of us who would have burned our own huts before we let a Roman soldier sit at our table, but not you, Daniel the coward."

Desperately Dan tried to remember, searching his mind for some small glimmer of events past. But there was nothing. If, as Orlenda had told him, Dan had been a simple farmer like the others, why would he have allowed the soldiers to come in his hut? Was it possible that some-how, in this act which he could not remember, he had rec-ognized the face of a friend-yet-to-be? Was it treachery to welcome a friend? Was it cowardice to refuse to fight when you held no personal grudge against an enemy?

Ambrose leaned down, his face close to Dan's, and his breath stank from the goat cheese still on his tongue. "I will tell you something more, coward, and this you will not forget: it was not the Romans who burned your hut, it was I. When word came that the patrol was inside, we set fire to the thatch ourselves, and as the soldiers came out, we attacked. It was I, the last of the Brigantes, who led the Picts; I, your neighbor, who burned you down, not the Romans, as my daughter believes. There is enough hate in me to burn down a hundred huts and the people in them if it would give the land once more to the Britons."

He straightened up, reached for the pitcher of mead beside him, and drank heavily. None of the other tribes-men joined him, but hung back a respectful distance away, watching.

"So now I see you managed to survive both the fire and the battle and are back to treachery once more; you have been to Eboracum," he said.

"No, Ambrose, I swear it."

"Then why so far from home? What brings you out here when there is battle about to be born?"

101

The other tribesmen moved in closer, curious about Dan's answer. All of the faces seemed fierce in the blue of their paint.

"Orlenda was frightened," Dan said, telling only half the truth. "She fears another attack by the patrol and asked me to come—to check the road and see if soldiers were about."

"You lie to me!" Ambrose raged and, lunging forward, yanked Dan up to his knees. Quickly the big hands searched his garments and seconds later, ripping at the corner of Dan's shirt, he found the silver denarius. He struck Dan across the face with the back of his hand.

"So they have chosen you to betray us," he said. "Even as you lied to me, the coin was hot against your leg. Did they give you a piece of silver the day you lured Nat away to the legion? And now they have paid you once again to do us harm." He spat at Dan. "A *friend*!" he hissed. "A *neighbor*!"

"I swear I mean no harm to your family," Dan protested, but Ambrose kicked him into silence.

Turning to his men, their leader said, "Do you see now why we fight? It's not enough that the Romans sail here in their galleys to add our land to the empire. It is not even enough that they recruit men beyond Rome with no grudge against us at all to come and fight their wars. But it is the final insult when they corrupt us from the inside and set us fighting against ourselves. For one silver denarius this fool would betray us, and within the week he would be marching too from Eboracum in plumed helmet, pleased to take his place behind the centurion." Ambrose stood up, and his eyes were terrible. "You will have no chance to march from Eboracum," he said, his face violet with rage, and wheeling about, spoke to the tribesmen: "Tie him to a tree and leave him. The wild dogs or the Roman soldiers will make short work of him, whichever finds him first. I will leave him to their fate. We will not soil our hands with any but Roman blood this night. We will keep ourselves for an enemy worth the battle."

Even as Dan was hauled over to an oak tree and tied with hemp to its trunk, he knew he could have saved himself. Even as he felt the rope cutting tightly against his wrists and around his ankles, he knew that if he told them about the centurion and what he had been commanded to do, it would go better for him. But he could not. The words jammed in his throat, like a lump that would go neither up nor down.

If Ambrose knew for a certainty that the soldiers believed themselves cut off and their situation to be desperate, he would move in at once. If he knew there were no more than thirty, he might even reward Dan for having refused to do the centurion's bidding. But the face of Joe Stanton haunted him—those eyes beneath the helmet.

Twice Dan opened his mouth, and twice the words would not come. And then the tribesmen disappeared, as stealthily as they had come, and the forest itself grew dark.

Terror rose up in him and would not go away. Now and then the stillness was broken with the grunt of an animal, the breaking of a twig, the call of a bird, the rustle of leaves overhead, only to have quiet descend once more. But the terror remained.

Dan tried to calculate how far he was from the hut. Ambrose had implied that he was still a long way off. Perhaps he had merely been walking in a circle. Even if he were able to free himself, he would not know which way to go in the dark.

An hour slipped by and then two, and his body ached with weariness, his hands numb from the pressure of the rope. He could hear the braying of wild dogs in the distance. Sometimes it seemed they were close at hand, and then their yelps and howls would recede once more. They had not yet caught his scent. Occasionally, too, he heard singing, faintly, and knew it to be the tribesmen. Whether the chant was a prayer, a call to battle, or a celebration of his death to come, he didn't know.

It was not the way he wanted to end his life, betwixt and between. He did not want to die having taken no stand at all. If only he could have believed fervently in the rightness of Rome, he could have rushed toward Eboracum, putting all his heart and strength into the mission—boldly, courageously. Then, had he been killed by the tribesmen along the way, someone, somewhere, would learn of it, and the story would be told throughout the fort and passed along to other soldiers yet to come—the story of the young farmer from the north of Briton who had lost his life in the service of the Emperor Honorius.

Or, if he believed in the cause of the tribesmen and, having disobeyed the centurion's command, had been caught once again by the soldiers, the news of his death would have spread from tribe to tribe all the way to Caledonia, and his name would be preserved for generations to come as the young Briton who defied Rome.

He was not destined to be a hero. Dying in this place, beneath this oak, he was held in contempt by Romans and tribesmen alike. There was no laurel wreath, he knew, for the one who refused to fight. Civilizations, the argument went, had crumbled for lack of conviction. What if everyone took his position? What if no one fought for any cause whatsoever?

The answer to that was simple. There would be no wars.

True, the argument would continue, but what if only some of the men felt that way? Should some fight and the others stay home?

It was not an argument easily answered. There was no

glory in refusing to go, no trumpets or banners for the men who stayed behind. Yet there was something deeper, and that was conscience. No trumpets could heal the heart if he killed a man he didn't know merely because he had been given an order. No medals, no banners, could soothe the mind after knowing that he had taken the life of another who had come into battle as frightened, confused, and empty of a reason for fighting as he had been.

If he went his whole life waiting until there were enough like him to take a stand, what kind of hero was that? If he kept silent, how would others, who felt the same, ever know? If civilization depended on mass murder to save it, was it worth the price? If society had to resort to barbarism to prevent barbarism, what then?

No matter what happened to him here in these woods on this night, Dan decided, no matter how he died, the news of his death would reach Orlenda, and she would know that he had been returning for her. It was enough that she knew.

A feeling of extreme drowsiness swept over him, sapping the strength that remained, kindling his wish to give up, to have done with the waiting. He thought of his parents and wondered how his death would affect them.

Would his death be final, however? If he had once lived in this time, in this place, hadn't he died already and been reborn back in Harrisburg? Was it possible there had been other times he had lived, other times he had died, and that he was called upon now and then to relive a piece of the past, to do something over that had been left undone? Is that why he remembered nothing that had happened before he had found himself standing outside Orlenda's hut?

A twig snapped again somewhere behind him. Dan turned quickly, trying to see through the blackness, looking for a quick glint of metal that would announce the arrival of the centurion. There was nothing, however, but darkness. And then he felt a tentative jerk on his hands, something touching them from behind, and he gave a short cry, clutching his fingers into fists against the anticipated teeth of an animal.

But it was no animal. In the next moment he felt the warmth of human flesh, the working of fingers, and he stood still, waiting, the pounding of his heart subsiding as he felt the hemp slacken. He was weak with relief. Could it possibly be Orlenda? Could he be closer to the hut than he had thought?

"Orlenda?" he whispered softly, but there was no reply, and he could tell, finally, from the roughness of the fingers against his own, that they were not those of a girl.

And then the rope fell loose—first around his wrists, then about his body and knees. There was the sound of someone breathing in front of him, then kneeling, working at the rope around his feet. Dan put out one hand to clasp this friend, and his fingers touched a hank of hair that felt stiff and chalky, standing straight up from the head. Jasper.

In another moment Dan was free, and his rescuer had gone. He could hear only the sound of his footsteps retreating into the forest, and so he followed, knowing that Jasper would lead him home.

It was at least another two hours before Dan recognized the clearing near the hut. Jasper disappeared as suddenly as he had come. All at once the footsteps simply ceased, and as Dan looked about in the faint light of a new moon, he saw that the young man had gone. And yet, not too far off, he heard a man's singing, a wavery utterance of Celtic syllables that drifted now closer, now further, upon the wind.

Dan waited, wondering, remembering the magpie that Jasper had brought to his mother for a Druid sacrifice here in this place—remembering, too, the singing of the tribesmen after his capture that very night.

He started when he saw the door to the hut open, the glow of the hearth shining through, and he crouched, ready to run, expecting Rose in her long cloak. A figure came swiftly out the door, shutting it softly behind her, and as it drew closer, Dan could see that it was Orlenda, with Rachel asleep in her arms. In spite of his fatigue, he felt strangely rejuvenated at the thought of the task ahead and hurried to meet her, lifting Rachel to his shoulder.

"I was so afraid something had happened," Orlenda said, grasping his hand quickly and leading him back into the trees.

"I came as quickly as I could," Dan said, "but I didn't think I would ever see you again."

Orlenda looked alarmed. "Why, Daniel? What is it?"

He told her all that had taken place, and when he reached the part about having been tied to a tree, Orlenda suddenly threw her arms around him, her relief mixing with his own, her head against his chest.

"That's what happened, then. I knew it, I knew!" She backed off as Rachel stirred, and they walked on, Orlenda holding tight to Dan's arm. "How did you get here?"

"It was Jasper. Somehow he found me and later, in the night, set me free. I followed the sound of his footsteps, and he was gone before I could thank him."

"Yes, it's like Jasper to do that for me. He knew, I think, that I was leaving. He says nothing to me, yet he seems to know everything. He can sense it. Some days when I'm gathering sticks in the forest, he comes up to me and helps, and I talk to him—like one talks to a pet, for he never answers. And yet I think he's answering all the time in his heart. When I heard him singing tonight, I felt he had something for me and came out. The something was you."

"Then he does sing."

"Oh, yes. It's a strange madness, Daniel. What he saw that day on the coast when my grandmother was killed is something that can never be washed from his mind. It is as though he can never trust people again, ever. He saves his voice for the forest—for the birds and the animals that know him."

"And yet it was Jasper who brought the magpie to your mother that night. It was Jasper who killed it."

"Yes, for Mother he will do even that. Jasper has a great fondness for other birds, but none at all for the magpie. Mother said that the day my grandmother died, there were four magpies on a branch just above her body. Jasper must have seen them too and ever since has associated them with death. They are the only thing in the forest that embody evil for him, the only creature on which he vents his rage." She shifted the basket to her other arm and clutched at the large goatskin she had thrown about her shoulders, which dragged on the ground behind.

"Your mother doesn't know that you left, then?" Dan asked.

"I'm not sure. It was very difficult to get away. For a long time she sat before the fire and held Rachel on her lap as though afraid to let her go. Then, when I lay down and she thought I was asleep, she came over and kissed me. I wanted to cry, Daniel—to put my head against her like a small child. But I thought it best to go on pretending. Had she known for certain we were leaving, she would have felt obligated to stop us."

"She'll miss you."

"Yes, but she wants us to be safe—wants Rachel to grow up where it's peaceful. Yet, who will there be to tell her whether we arrive in Eboracum safely? Who will there be to tell her when we are on our way to Deva?"

"Perhaps it will be Jasper. Perhaps somehow he will get the message through."

"Maybe so."

It was difficult traveling with Rachel, for she was bundled in all of the clothes that Orlenda could put on her, making her slight body heavy and hard to hold. When she stirred finally and began to murmur, Orlenda took her from Dan and set her on the ground.

"Rachel," she said, shaking her gently. "You must walk now, and later we will carry you again. Are you awake, Rachel? Are you listening?"

The small girl weaved slightly as though she might fall, then righted herself, her eyes half open.

"Listen, Rachel, we are going for a very long walk to a place where there's no fighting. You will get tired, but you must keep very, very still. Do you think you can do it? Can we trust you to go with us?"

The child opened her eyes wider with effort, looked at

Dan, then back at her sister. "Where's Mother?"

"Mother needed to stay. She couldn't come, but perhaps some day we will send for her. She loves you very much and wants you to be safe. But you must be very brave and strong to go with us."

"I *am* brave."

"Good. Let's hurry now, and when you absolutely can't walk any more, we will rest. Daniel is here to help us."

They moved on in the direction that Dan had gone that morning, and he went first, holding the brambles aside so that Orlenda and her sister could pass. He kept more to the east, however, hoping to avoid entirely the places where he had encountered the tribesmen and soldiers before. The countryside alternated between wild waterless hills and forlorn, swampy places.

Sometimes, when the path was particularly rocky and Orlenda tired, she would walk beside Dan, leaning her head on his shoulder, and he would brace her with his arm, delighting in the feel of her soft hair next to his cheek. Other times it was Rachel who tired. Afraid to cry out, she would simply hang back, exhausted. Then they would all sit down to rest, or Dan would carry the little girl again in his arms.

"Look," Orlenda whispered when they came out on the edge of the moor. "The moon is shining without a cloud over its face. That's a good sign."

"Perhaps," said Dan, "but it shows the soldiers their way as well. We must be careful to walk here in the shadow of the trees."

"Oh, can't we rest, Daniel? Sleep a little?" Orlenda pleaded. "I've not slept at all this night, and neither have you."

Her very words seemed to bring on his own fatigue, to open the floodgates for all the weariness he had suppressed. His arms ached with the effort of carrying Rachel, who had fallen asleep once more on his shoulder.

"Maybe for a few hours, Orlenda, just until it's light," he told her, and sighing with relief, she unfastened the goatskin about her shoulders and laid it on the ground. Rachel was placed under the protection of some pine branches, and Orlenda sat down on the goatskin, patting the place beside her for Dan. She opened her basket and took out the meat and cheese.

"Look," she said, showing him her treasure. "Salt! I brought some just for you."

Dan tried to eat slowly, knowing that a little would have to satisfy him. They must make the food last. Chewing each mouthful longer than usual made it seem as though there was more, and perhaps he could trick his stomach. But Orlenda had no such scruples. She tore at her piece of roasted bird, smacking her lips and sucking at the bone long after the meat was gone. Then, daintily, she wiped her fingers on the grass and lay down, her lids heavy with sleep.

Dan put the cork back in the flask and lay down beside the girl, encircling her with his arms to keep her warm. There was enough of the goatskin to cover them barely and, thus wrapped, the warmth of her body relaxed him.

How precious the girl was to him, Dan thought as he held her, trying to cover her back with his hands to ward off the chill wind. How good to have someone else to care for, to be concerned about. If only he could reach the west with her, and if it could indeed be the place of peace that her mother remembered.

The morning was gray, overcast with thick, swirling clouds. Vapors rose from the earth, veiling the trees around. Dan's leg felt numb, and he cautiously stretched it, wiggling his toes. Feeling him stir, Orlenda opened her eyes, blinked at the mist, and closed them again.

"They will attack," she said simply.

"Who?"

"The tribesmen. Fog is their friend, for they know the land well—every bog, every rock. When there is mist, then there is sure to be a battle." She rolled over, checked Rachel who was curled in a small heap beneath the tree, and then went back to the warmth of Dan's arms. "Isn't it strange, Daniel, that something as beautiful as mist can be so deadly? I have thought of that many times. I've thought how the world would be with no people in it—just sun and rain and mist and snows—so quiet and peaceful."

Dan stroked her hair and said nothing.

"I wonder why it is I had to be born at this time—why I couldn't have been a child a hundred years ago, in the land of my mother's people. I wouldn't have known about war then. I would have had a husband and children and could have watched them grow up strong and happy. I wouldn't have had to live as I do now, with one brother a soldier for Rome and my father a Brigante—knowing every day of my life that I might some day see my mother or my sister slaughtered before my eyes."

She rolled over on her back and studied her hand, which she held out in front of her, marveling at the way her fingers became blurred in the fog. "I had a dream once—a strange dream—about a new kind of war. I dreamed that instead of soldiers with daggers and spears, the Romans sent a magpie with a torch in its beak. When the bird dropped it over a village, all the huts went up in fire at the same time, quickly. I knew I would die in the dream, but I was happy because we were all dying together—my mother and sister and I. Even my father and Nat and Jasper were there. We didn't have to watch soldiers forming with their shields together, advancing like a wall of metal, or listen to their war shouts. We didn't have to see pirates crawling up a cliff, daggers at their sides. We didn't have to scream and run and try to hide the children. There wasn't the awful terror of having a soldier look our way, knowing that his knife would be next against our throats. We didn't have to flee into the forest hearing his footsteps behind us. We all went together and were so happy that it was not more horrible. That is the kind of war I would like, if there must be any at all."

"Orlenda, that's a terrible thing to say. You don't know what you're talking about," Dan said earnestly. "Such a war would be even more horrible because it would be so impersonal. The destruction would be unbelievable. Both forts and temples would be leveled to the ground, and the survivors would eat each other for lack of food. With magpies flying about carrying torches, you would not even need soldiers. The birds could fly far and wide and bring devastation on all of Britain, even those tribes that wanted peace. Don't ever think such a thing. It would be hideous."

Orlenda shook her head. "I can tell that you have never known what it is to meet the enemy up close, to see their fierce faces and hear their cries. You've never known what it is like for a soldier to select you from all the others and give chase. If there were such a thing as magpies carrying torches and dropping them on villages, it would not be as though the magpie were against you personally. The bird would simply be doing something it was trained to do, with no knowledge of the consequences. Those who could escape would, without soldiers tracking them down to slit every remaining throat. It would be more like attacking a village than attacking its people—a tribe, rather than the men in it. Can't you understand?"

"It would be only the beginning of even more terrible things. Wars would become bigger and bigger, not just one patrol against a tribe, but lands against lands, whole peoples against peoples. All of Britain would be ravaged, with nothing left for the survivors."

"No," said Orlenda. "This, now, is the worst of all possible times. I wish I lived hundreds of years in the past, or hundreds of years in the future. But I can't." She put her arms around Dan again, and he could sense that she was crying softly.

He pressed her to him and kissed her forehead. "If you were born in any other time, Orlenda—if you had been conceived even a moment earlier or later—you would not be the person you are now."

"That's surely a strange thing to say."

"But it's true. You may be conceived in the best of times or the worst of times, but it is *your* moment, your chance at life."

She ran her finger lightly over his nose and lips. "There are times, Daniel, when you don't talk like one of us. You talk as though you have lived in faraway places and studied with the scholars."

"I am a very wise man," Dan joked, anxious to brighten her mood and strengthen her for the long journey that was yet to come.

"Very wise or very foolish," she said, getting to her feet. "You told Nat tales that took him away from us. And now you're taking me away also, to the land of the west. Oh, how my father must hate you." She turned her back on him suddenly, faced the west, and lifted her arms high above her head, fingers stretching as if to touch the sky. Almost inaudibly she repeated a Celtic prayer, which Dan could only partially understand. Then she turned to him again.

"May we go in peace, without trouble," she said, and they rolled up the goatskin and divided the morning's bread.

They made their way single file through the thicket—Dan in the lead, Rachel between them—stopping now and then to take the burrs off the small girl's footwrappings, or to drink from the flask in the basket. Dan kept his ear to the wind, an eye to the sun, trying to stay east of the forest where the soldiers were surrounded. The fog only seemed to increase, the sky became darker, and then they heard it, the sound of battle.

"Daniel!" Orlenda clung to him, and Rachel, bewildered, grasped her sister's cloak.

Dan held them both, crouching there in the yew bushes. He was astonished that he had so misjudged their direction and that they were now so close to the fighting as to hear it. Every now and then the air was pierced with the far-off shout of a man's voice, commanding the others, and though Dan could not make out the words, he knew that it must be the voice of the centurion. There was also the sound of armor—of swords striking shields—echoing along through the forest, and the frenzied birdlike calls of the tribesmen.

Orlenda began to weep, and Dan could think of nothing to say that would be comforting. There would be no winners in this battle, not for her. She hugged her sister to her. "It's for this reason we're going away, Rachel. It's so that you and I will never have to listen to the sounds of fighting ever again."

But the little girl sobbed loudly, too terrified to go on, so Dan picked her up in his arms and carried her once more, and Orlenda followed, stumbling along behind him.

It could not have been over five minutes later that the noise of battle stopped. Dan paused, listening, wondering if it was possible that they had gotten so far away so quickly. But the silence was absolute. There were no lingering sounds of metal clashing, no cries, no horses' whinnies, no shouts, not even a thud of footsteps, which he might expect from a retreating patrol. Was it possible, he wondered, that every man had been slaughtered—that the soldiers, knowing they were surrounded and that defeat was certain, took as many tribesmen as they could with them? Did Ambrose and the centurion fall first and their men follow, or did the men fall and then Ambrose and Joe Stanton fight to their deaths there among the trees?

"You know," Orlenda said finally, "my father told me once that he had met this centurion who goes out on patrol. He said that he came upon him at a spring in the woods. The centurion had taken his sandals off and was washing his feet when my father found him. There were no other soldiers about, no other tribesmen, and there could have been a battle, a fight to the death, but there wasn't. If my father had killed the centurion, his troops would have retreated in confusion. And if the centurion had killed my father, my people would have fled into the hills of Caledonia."

"What happened, then?"

"It was very curious. Each knew at once who the other was—a man against whom he had been fighting all these years. Yet neither reached for his weapon. My father waded into the water beside the centurion, and they washed their feet together. They did not speak. He said that they looked deep into each other's eyes, and he felt then, at that moment, that their fates were sealed, as if by the water itself, and that whatever happened to one would happen also to the other. If my father died today, the centurion died with him, of that I am sure."

They went on, hurrying faster so that if the fighting resumed they would not be caught up in it. By the time the sun was full up, the fog had lifted. Dan judged that very soon they should be in sight of Eboracum, and that possibly, over the rise of the ridge ahead, they would see the fort below and the settlement there on the banks of the Ouse.

They sat down to rest, to eat the cheese and drink the wine that remained in the basket. Rachel was glad to be stopping awhile and went skipping about the meadow, plucking wild flowers here and there and bringing them back to her sister. To amuse her, Orlenda fashioned the flowers into a braid for Rachel to wear on her head, and the small girl laughed with delight as the braid lengthened, picking more and more flowers to put in her sister's lap.

Dan watched them and realized suddenly that he had seen this once before—the meadow, the flowers, the smile on the small girl's face, and Orlenda's slim brown fingers, fashioning the braid.

"What is it, Daniel?" Orlenda asked, looking at him quizzically.

"I have known you before, I'm sure of it," he said. "I saw you sitting this way once, just as you are now."

Orlenda laughed, showing her white teeth, and tucked her ankles under her. "You speak strangely, Daniel—but you have always been strange. Perhaps that's why I like you."

"I've always been strange?" Dan repeated. "And how long was that?"

She laughed at his teasing. "Since we discovered your hut in the forest. We had always thought it an overgrown hill of gorse and ivy, and then one day we saw you in it, as though you had sprung up out of the earth overnight." She sighed. "It was good to have a neighbor, especially after my father left."

Dan said nothing, trying to fit the pieces together. He had arrived at the end of the fourth century, then, quite suddenly, and he felt more certain than ever that he had been called back for a reason; the reason was Orlenda. He silently set to work on his leg wrappings, binding them more tightly about his calf, adjusting the hide that bound his foot.

There was the feel of the earth vibrating beneath him, and then a sound becoming more and more distinct, like running feet. Dan crawled over to the rock next to Orlenda, ready to spring as the footsteps seemed almost upon them. A moment later a young man, gasping breathlessly, appeared at the top of the rock and, with a cry, fell down among them, lying motionless. Orlenda screamed and covered her mouth, and Dan saw that it was Nat.

He crawled over to him, fearful that he was dying. But when he examined the wounds, he found only deep scratches, and Orlenda sank back, eyes closed with relief. It was fright and exhaustion that had overpowered her brother. Rachel, hardly recognizing this member of the family who had been away so long, sat off to one side, watching warily.

Dan got the flask and held it to Nat's lips. Gradually, as the ale slid down his throat, the color returned to Nat's face and his breathing became slower, but he could not seem to stop the shaking.

"Orlenda," he kept saying, "I can't believe this. Surely Brigantia has heard my prayers. How is it you're here?"

"We'll tell you later," Orlenda promised. "What has happened?"

"I've deserted," Nat said. "I'm done for, Orlenda. I'll be killed no matter who finds me now. I threw off my armor as I was running, but I've no place to go. I'll be stoned if I go into Eboracum, killed by my own people if I try to go home."

"Is Ambrose alive?" Dan asked.

Nat lay back again and took several more deep breaths. "The strangest battle that was ever fought," he said. He took the flask and drank until it was drained. "The tribesmen attacked. They had us surrounded. I recognized my father's call. I knew, even that morning when I saw the mist, that we would be ambushed before sunup. I warned the centurion and we were ready, but they greatly outnumbered us. And I didn't want to fight.

"They came from all sides. Father had organized them well. There were men from many tribes—Picts and Scots and Saxons and Jutes and Angles—as though he had traveled through all the north provinces enlisting men for his army. Yet it was more of a contest than a fight. Easily they could have killed us, despite our weapons, but it was like a jousting—a standoff. When I saw my father enter the woods, my own heart turned to ice. I knew I could not fight him, nor his men either, my own people. Other soldiers, I know, felt the same, and the tribesmen as well. On all sides, cousin recognized cousin, and the fighting was—would you believe it—polite? Father shouted and cursed, yet still his men seemed to be holding back.

"But now and then a man fell—a sword had struck in earnest, and at the sight of those there on the ground, the fighting became more intense."

"Then?" asked Orlenda, frantic for details.

"Then our mother came into the woods carrying a torch."

"*Mother?*"

"You will never believe this. It was a sight that will be forever in front of my eyes. I have never seen her look so tall or regal. On she came, slowly, her long cloak trailing, her arms stretched to the sky, a burning torch in one hand, and strange sounds coming from her throat. Like a huge bird she swept into the clearing, and the men on all sides fell back, staring. In and out she weaved, frightening the Romans who cried out at the sight of a woman in their ranks, and our centurion commanded us to let her pass safely through. The tribesmen, of course, would not harm her, and even Ambrose was startled by her coming. There were many on both sides who knew her. It was though she were an omen, a signal, to call off the fight. It was then that I slipped away. I can't believe the tribesmen will let the soldiers go, though. Never before have they managed to surround an entire patrol and capture the centurion also, but I didn't wait to find out."

Dan watched him, stunned by what he had said. Nat was neither child nor man, merely a youngster in Roman sandals and a green kilt. He had the features of both his parents—the thick unruly hair of his father, the thin lips and fine profile of his mother, and he sat up now, struggling to remove the dagger in his pouch, to throw it away and have done with his stint at soldiering.

"I thought I was running toward Eboracum, but everything is turned around. Why are you here? Is the hut close by?"

"We're leaving too," Orlenda told him. "Daniel is taking us to the land of Mother's people. Rachel deserves the chance to grow up in a place of peace. I couldn't take the fighting—even the threat of fighting—any longer, Nat, but I knew that Mother would never come with us, not with Father and Jasper still at home, and worrying so about you."

"It sickens me that I have caused her so much grief," said Nat.

"I think it's because we left, Rachel and I, that she did what she has done this morning," Orlenda mused. "She has lost all of her children, in one way or another, to war. Perhaps she felt there was no one else to stop the fighting but herself."

"And perhaps she'll succeed for now," Dan told them hopefully.

"But only for now," said Orlenda. "Peace will never come so easily. Why is it, do you suppose, when people could share all things with each other, they choose to fight instead? Was there ever a war that brought about a lasting peace? Or did it only start another, in a different place?"

But Nat was not interested in her speculations. "Listen, Orlenda, there may be other soldiers returning. If the battle has really stopped, the centurion will lead his men back to Eboracum for more forces and supplies. We can't be found together or they will kill you too. Go on now, quickly."

"No." Orlenda was firm. "You are to come with us, Nat."

"Orlenda, you must be mad. You know what they do to deserters."

126

"Then we'll hide you."

"You *are* mad! I can never return to Eboracum."

"Then you and I will go on together, Nat," said Dan, "because I can't be discovered there either. The soldiers would be no more kind to me." He turned to Orlenda. "We'll see you safely to the settlement and leave you and Rachel while we look for the land beyond Deva. When we find it, if it's all you say it is, we'll come back for you."

And so, with the high rise of the last ridge looming before them, they started on again, silent in the events of the morning.

Dan's calculations were right, for when they at last reached the top of the hill, staying next to the thicket where they would not be so visible from behind, they could see—far off in the distance—the wall of the fortress and the beginning of a civilian settlement across the River Ouse, which ran through the heart of Eboracum.

"What will you do when you get to the city, Orlenda?" Nat asked. "How do you know they'll let you in?"

"I can't imagine that anyone could be so heartless as to turn away a young girl and her sister," Orlenda answered. "I'll tell them that I am a daughter of the countryside, a peace-loving Briton, and that I am sick of all the fighting in the north and wish to be a housemaid. Rachel will help me. We will earn a small bag of silver, and when you come back for us, we'll have something to start with when we set up a home beyond Deva."

"Do you really believe there's a land out there?" Nat asked her.

"If we don't look for it," Orlenda said in answer, "we'll never know."

Nat took his turn carrying Rachel and went on ahead, but Orlenda turned and embraced Dan one last time.

"I learned long ago that it was bad luck to say goodbye, so this is not a goodbye, Daniel. It is my very deep thanks for coming with us, for protecting us, and for all you may need to do for Nat on the way."

Dan kissed her, wishing that it were he and Orlenda who were going on, and Nat and Rachel who would stay.

"It was you who took me in when I stood shivering outside your hut," he reminded. "You're the one to be thanked. Your happiness means a great deal to me, Orlenda. You know that." He was moved to see tears glistening in her dark eyes.

"Yes, I know that," she said. "May the gods be with you in Deva and show you the way to the west. If it's peaceful there, as Mother said, come for us. If it's not. . . ." She stopped, uncertain.

"I will come back for you regardless," Dan promised. "Wherever you are, it's home."

She left him swiftly, and he saw her wipe her sleeve

across her eyes. She took Rachel from Nat and was bidding her brother farewell when there was the sound of horse's hoofs on the earth behind them. Nat quickly leaped back into the bushes beside Dan. It was time now for Orlenda to make her bid to enter the city. Dan's heart beat fiercely, frightened that the retreating soldiers might take their frustration out on a defenseless young woman. Orlenda's beauty only made the situation more perilous.

The soldiers were some paces away, however, and did not see the two girls standing at the edge of the woods. Dan watched in fascination at the disheartened retreat. First to come into view was a Roman soldier on horseback and then behind, soldiers in twos, walking side by side. They looked neither to the right nor left, but trudged on in silence, heads down. They were small men, no more than five feet tall, their faces grimy and stubbled for lack of a shave. Their uniforms were shoddily made—the skirts, or kilts, in various shades of green—not at all the splendid issues of Rome. They all wore the same helmets and carried short swords on the right-hand side, like oversized daggers.

The horses, also, were not the slim, quick chargers that Dan might have imagined, but great cart horses, and they too looked exhausted, for each step they took seemed a strain upon their sweating bodies.

When they had all passed, Orlenda stepped out upon

the moor with Rachel, drawing her shawl about her, and prepared to follow after them. At that moment, however, there was another sound of hoofs close at hand and still another horse came along, this one so close to the edge of the thicket that Dan and Nat could have reached through the branches and touched it. Sitting astride it was the Roman centurion, and seeing Orlenda, he pulled back and brought the horse to a halt.

Orlenda whirled around, the breeze catching her shawl.

The centurion sat silently, watching the girls, and it was Orlenda who stepped toward him.

"Please," she said, "I ask permission to follow your soldiers into Eboracum. My sister and I are fleeing the countryside and wish to find work in the city."

"You do not need my permission," the centurion said, moving his horse forward a little. "It's only the fort where you cannot pass. Whose daughter are you?"

"My father has been gone a long time," Orlenda said, avoiding the question. "In the north we're surrounded by tribesmen and would seek the peace of Eboracum."

The centurion's face seemed more gentle. He had turned his horse at such an angle that Dan could see the man's profile well. How strange to see Joe Stanton here in this place. How odd, too, that only Dan seemed able to recall their friendship in York. Unlike Joe and Orlenda and

Ambrose and Rose, Dan saw the connections somehow, but possibly there was a reason. Perhaps, in remembering, his mission became more urgent, his effort more certain.

"What can you do, girl?" the centurion asked. "Do you bake? Do you sing?"

"I bake very decently, sir, and sing badly, but my sister bakes nothing and sings all day."

The centurion smiled. "So you go together, then, is that it? Like a pair of birds?"

"Yes, sir."

"Get on," the centurion said, and motioned to his horse. "I will see you safely into Eboracum, and perhaps one of the soldiers' wives will keep you in her house."

With both relief and anxiety, Dan watched as the centurion leaned down, extending his hand, and helped swing first Rachel, then Orlenda, onto the horse in front of him. As the big animal moved on over the moor, only the back of the soldier was visible and, fluttering out from one side, the fragile edge of Orlenda's shawl.

"What do you think?" Dan said at last to Nat as they stood there, motionless, watching. "Will he be good to her?"

"The centurion is an honorable man, I can tell you that," said Nat. "He would not let his men harm her, just as he did not let them hurt my mother when she walked into battle this morning. It's often crossed my mind that the wrong man was made centurion. He's brave and he speaks with courage; the men respect and obey him; but—when you look in his eyes, you sometimes feel that he has no heart for war."

"What will happen to him when he gets back to Eboracum?"

"I don't know. I've heard the soldiers tell stories of the way it used to be when the fort was new and the soldiers were fresh and the Ninth Legion had just moved up from Lindum. Discipline was strict then, and punishment severe. If a legion acted with cowardice in battle, every tenth man was stoned to death. It would have been unthinkable once not to fight to the death, no matter how outnumbered. Soldiers who deserted either lost their own lives or fled to the highlands where they lived out their days with the tribesmen. But now . . . I have heard the centurion say that Rome has all but forgotten us. It has problems enough in its eastern empire. That's why there is little heart for going out on patrol among the tribesmen. The men have no taste for it. I don't know what will happen to the centurion after this morning. Perhaps he will convince the Chief of the Legion that we waste our time and our men by protecting Eboracum from the north people. Better to give it back, perhaps, and protect the peace."

"What do you know about Deva and the land beyond?"

"I know nothing."

"I'm afraid for Orlenda, afraid that she expects a land that never was."

"Yet we can't stay here."

"So there's really no choice."

They went deeper into the woods so that they could pass by Eboracum unseen, hoping to pick up the road, if there was one, on the other side. Nat led the way, stumbling on toward a small stream that ran in a gully below. When they reached the clear water, he laid down on the bank and greedily drank from it, scooping up the water with one hand to reach his mouth all the more quickly.

Dan also lay down on the bank to drink and realized as he did so that he was exhausted. Except for the few hours of sleep he had taken in the arms of Orlenda, he had not slept at all for two days. The battle, for the time being, was over. Orlenda, for better or worse, was on her way to Eboracum with Rachel, and although both he and Nat would probably be put to death were they recognized near the fort, he did not feel any great need to hurry. He felt his limbs relax.

His hand was almost too tired to scoop up the water. He lay, instead, with his cheek against the damp earth, one hand lazily in the stream, feeling the current coursing through his fingers. He wanted nothing so much now as a chance to sleep, not even the taste of coolness on his tongue.

"It would be good if we could get around Eboracum before nightfall," Nat was saying. "The road will be well marked beyond the city, with a broad swathe of forest felled on either side to protect the soldiers from ambush. We must not walk on the road directly, but can follow at a distance in the brush."

But Dan could not seem to move, could not even stir. His muscles, his nerves, all begged for rest, and he gave in, letting his body sink gratefully into the grass on the bank. Somewhere above in the trees, he heard the raucous call of a magpie, but even that did not stir him, and he slept.

6

DARKNESS AND DAMP and the icy shroud of swirling water. Flashes of light, of heat, of voices and babbling mingled with mists and vapors.

Dan felt as though he were sliding rapidly down a muddy hill toward a precipice, and he could hear now the sound of water tumbling over the cliffs below him. He put out one hand to stop himself, to grasp whatever there was left of life, a few seconds more of time before that plunge into nothingness. His hand grasped only pebbles, but the splash of water on his face jolted him into opening his eyes.

His cheek lay against the damp earth as it had when he'd gone to sleep, and his left hand was still in the water. At first he felt that his back was broken, for there were pains in every bone, as though he had suffered some horrible beating. Slowly, slowly, he lifted his head and looked around for Nat, but he saw instead the face of Jasper.

He startled and tried to sit up, and the young man drew back, then turned and looked at the woman who was waiting anxiously there on the cellar stairs.

Dan stared at them incredulously. His grandmother was coming down the rest of the way now, a step at a time, and she held her old blue bathrobe tightly around her. Lonnie squatted on his heels, his eyes intense, saying nothing.

Dan inched upright until he was sitting, testing one muscle at a time. Everything about him seemed to work, with effort. Daylight poured through the opening in the cellar wall, exchanging places with the stream that moved swiftly out toward the creek beyond.

"Lad, are you all right?" Blossom asked, padding quickly over to him in her slippers. "Lord, what a scare you gave me! I looked the house over for you this morning and couldn't find you. Your bed was untouched. And then, when I opened the cellar door and saw you lying here, I screamed for Lonnie and he come running. . . . We were about to call for the doctor. Fell down the stairs, that's what you did!"

Dan looked up at her blankly.

"Look at you!" Blossom cried, as though to confirm it. "Clothes all torn, arms bruised. . . ."

Dan examined himself groggily. He wore the same

shirt he had been wearing the day before, the same jeans and boots. . . . And there was his watch, safely on his wrist, with the Roman coin hidden in the band. He leaned forward, arms on his knees, and rested his head against them. His body was numb with weariness.

Bee was moving slowly around the basement. She stopped and picked up the torn pillowcase in which Dan had imprisoned the magpie. "And what's this?" she said, looking first at it, then at Dan.

He did not have the strength to explain it.

Suddenly Blossom wheeled about and faced Lonnie. "I want the truth now," she said, and her voice had lost its gentleness. "There was no fighting between you, was there?"

Lonnie stood up, back tense, face gray. "No, ma'am."

"He's right, Bee," Dan said quietly. "Lonnie had nothing to do with it."

"Well, *that's* a blessing," Blossom said, the old spark returning to her voice. "What happened, then?"

"The magpie was in my room." He hesitated, then hedged the truth. "I was trying to get it out, so I caught it in my pillowcase."

"A bird in that!" Blossom said incredulously. "Land sakes, why didn't you just open the window and take a broom to it? Look at your shirt! That bird put up a fight."

"I just didn't think," Dan said.

"So what were you doing down here?"

Dan realized that nothing he could say would make any sense. He shook his head. "It's . . . hard to remember," he told her.

Blossom looked at him strangely, then turned suddenly and started back upstairs.

"Then that proves it, you see. It's the way it is after a fall. You don't remember what went before. Come on up and let's have a look at you in the daylight. Some food in your stomach should help, I would think."

Lonnie, however, hung back.

"Can you walk it?" he asked.

"I think so." Dan rose up to a squat, wobbling at first, and crouched for a moment with his hand on the floor, then stood.

"Tell me something," he said to Lonnie, for he had to know. "Did they get there safely?"

Lonnie's eyes met his, and they seemed like dark fire in a sun-browned face—as though, if Dan got too close to them, the sparks would burn. "I don't know what you're on about."

"Your sisters," Dan said.

"They haven't gone no place yet."

Dan closed his eyes for a moment, as though somehow he might bring it all back. As if by closing out the scene there in the cellar, he might conjure Orlenda up again, might hear her voice, might see her riding off with the centurion. When he opened them again, he was surprised to find himself alone, for Lonnie had gone back upstairs and outside.

Bee was waiting for him in the kitchen.

"Sit down, Dan, and I'll give you some coffee. It will help clear your head."

He did as she asked.

"I was about to call your mother this morning, that was the fright you gave me," she said, putting the cup before him. "I'm glad I didn't have to. She doesn't need another worry on her right now. Has this ever happened before— your falling?"

How could he explain it? How could he tell her he remembered leaning over the spring where the magpie had disappeared? Should he let her in on everything and see what she could make of it?

"No," he said finally, "it never happened before."

He could see the worry lines in her face grow deeper, the little knot of creases above the brows regroup themselves into the look of fear that occasionally crossed her face.

"Are you having any other symptoms you've not told me about, Dan? It's no good keeping it all in, you know. What will happen will happen."

He knew then that she was talking about Huntington's

disease and sought to reassure her, to go along with her version of the accident.

"No, Bee. I think I was just tired—missed a step or something. In any case, I'm all right now. No concussions, no broken bones. I'll just take it easy today and get back to the painting tomorrow."

But he found he could not dismiss it so lightly.

"Tell me the truth now, Dan," Blossom said. "What were you doing in the cellar?"

He watched her face and decided to tell part of it, anyway. "There's something strange about that bird, Bee; about why it's here. I thought maybe it had to do with the old gypsy's face—your great-grandfather's face, I mean—there in the stream. So I took the bird down there to let it out. . . ."

She frowned quizzically. "And?"

He shrugged. That was as far as he would take it. "Then, I don't know. I fell, I guess, and the bird got away. You know the rest."

She accepted it. Her eyes began to crinkle at the corners. "Lord, Dan, I don't know who's crazier, you or me. A face in the water, a bird in a pillowcase. . . . If your mother knew what was going on here, she'd lock us both up."

They laughed together, and Dan knew that the questioning was over.

"I was afraid you'd be angry that I let Lonnie come

down in the cellar," Bee said. "But I was so *frightened*, Dan. . . . you lying down there like you were dead or something. Someone had to help."

"That's okay," Dan told her. "I've no grudge against Lonnie."

Blossom got up then and stood before the old mirror above the sink, braiding her hair. Dan watched her reflection in the glass.

"I'm glad. If you and Lonnie had been fighting, it would worry me to death," she said.

"Don't think any more about it, Bee. He's okay. I was just concerned because you hired someone you didn't know."

"You're right, I didn't, but he reminded me of somebody I knew a long time ago, and I think I wanted to make amends." The bent fingers worked slowly, twisting and plaiting the long strands of white hair. Blossom did not look at Dan directly, but kept her eyes on herself. "When I was a young bride, you see, and my Thomas brought me here, he hired him a young man named Jeremy Dawson to help him out in the fields. The Dawsons were a migrant family, who followed the seasons—and every year the father would arrive with all his brood in a big green farm wagon pulled by two horses. They always camped for a spell at Mt. Wolf, across the river, and every morning them boys would go out working the farms both sides the Susquehanna. Wherever they could get work—for a day or a week or a month—that's where the boys would go."

Blossom came back over to the table and stood behind her chair, her hands gripping its back, eyes down, the pink again in her cheeks. "Jeremy—well, he was a decent lad, but not quite right, it seemed to me. Silent like. 'Slow-witted,' some of the folks hereabout called him. Well, as I said, I was a young bride and not used to summer on a farm. I didn't know that my Thomas would be out in the fields from dawn to dark, and so tired when he got in that there wasn't a lot of time for me. And it was to make Thomas jealous that I told him after a time that Jeremy had been sweet-talking me behind his back—poor, slow-witted Jeremy, who hadn't even opened his mouth to me since the day he came. And Thomas let him go. Just up and told him the next morning not to come back. It didn't turn out the way I had thought."

Relieved of her confession, Blossom pulled out her chair from the table and sat down. "It was only later, when I heard people talking in town about the Dawson boys, that I found out about Jeremy. It was 1918, and a year before, they told me, the lad had taken a real shock. His brother was killed in the war, and Jeremy never got over it. From then on, they said, he hardly talked to anybody, and there I was, putting blame on a man who had already suf-fered enough." She shook her head, cheeks pinker still.

"You were young, Bee," Dan told her.

"That's true, but what I wouldn't have given to undo that lie. When the Dawsons were about again the next summer, I wanted with all my heart to tell Thomas that I was mistaken about Jeremy, but I couldn't. It would have sounded as if I wanted more of that sweet talk, and if I admitted that I had lied, well . . . Thomas wouldn't have taken kindly to that at all. And so I said nothing. Do you know, Dan, that there is more harm done by good people who do nothing than by the bad ones themselves? I've thought of that many times. I always wondered if that was why I never bore children till I was in my late thirties—if that was my punishment. Instead of having babes about to keep me company when Thomas was off in the fields, I had nobody at all. And now—to find out that there was a sickness in the family, that Brian and his sister might get it yet. . . . Well, it does make me wonder. That's why, when Lonnie appeared at my door this summer and said his name was Dawson—and him the very image of Jeremy—I knew he was related somehow, a son or a grandson, maybe, sent to me to make my peace. And so I hired him. Now you know the story."

Dan sat very still, putting together pieces that seemed connected somehow, yet in wildly improbable ways that Blossom knew nothing of.

"Did you ever ask Lonnie about Jeremy, Bee?"

"No. I never had the courage."

"Where does he come from every morning? From across the river?"

"I don't know, Dan. I suppose he does. I just never asked. He shows up at breakfast and leaves again at four. I pay him by the day, and that's the way we've left it. I never asked how long he'd stay, and he never asked how long I'd want him. It's just one of those situations, it seems, where it's best not to know."

Dan lay on his bed, staring across at the picture of the sinking ship above the bureau—the billowy clouds, the swell of the waves, the listing of the ship, the men clinging to the side. . . . That was the state of his mind: confusion, havoc, and panic. Outside, the sky was dark and threatening, like the sky in the picture, and the air had cooled off sharply, leaving a damp clammy chill to his skin.

Slowly he felt along his ribs, his arms. There were scattered bruises and pains, very much like those he would have had if he had tumbled down the cellar stairs. Was it possible that this was what had really happened, this and nothing more? Is this the way it would be then, his mind playing tricks? Would he go on seeing things that weren't there, hearing voices no other ear could detect, convinced in his madness that he was right? Would he be so overcome with suspicion that he would not even know that he was sick?

He got up and moved slowly across the room to the

mirror, staring at the gaunt face before him. Suppose he *had* tumbled down the stairs and had rolled, unconscious, to the edge of the stream. Suppose he *had* only imagined that he had let the magpie out of the pillowcase and had seen it disappear into the spring. Then why, when he awakened, was the bird gone? Was it possible that Lonnie had come during the night and released it? Or that the bird had freed itself and flown out through the opening in the wall?

He touched one hand to his face and moved it slowly across the bruise on his cheekbone. And then he saw something else—a small piece of lavender-gray caught in a lock of his hair. He grasped it with his fingers and lifted it out, and his breath leaped as he examined it there in his hands: heather.

A strange relief flooded through him. His mind was not going after all, not yet. He *had* been away last night. He could not explain it, but somehow it had happened.

He thrust it in his pocket and went out to the barn to find Lonnie. He had to see him; had to know.

The sky was blacker still and a brisk wind played at the poplar trees standing in a line beyond the shed, tossing them first one way, then the other. The doors at both ends of the barn had been shut, as though anticipating a storm, and the snorting and stomping down at the far end told him that the horse was in.

"Lonnie?"

Dan waited there inside the door in the darkness. He scanned the gray lumps of the haymow, looking for the pinpoint of yellow that meant a match, sniffing for the familiar fragrance of Lonnie's pipe. Then he heard a voice behind him say, "Dan . . ." and he whirled about, one hand outstretched to protect himself.

There was no need. Lonnie was crouching over by the harnesses that had hung on the wall untouched since Dan's grandfather had died. He was working on the blades of the hand-propelled cultivator, scraping off the rust. "The grandmother want me for something?" he asked.

Dan hoisted himself up on the rail of the adjoining stall and leaned against the post. "No, I just wanted to talk. . . ." He stopped, groping for words, and finally shrugged. "I just wanted to say I haven't been very civil to you, and I'm sorry about it."

Lonnie stopped wiping the blades for a moment, looked at Dan curiously, and then smiled a little. "Didn't do me no harm that I can see."

"Just the same. . . ." said Dan.

Lonnie worked on in silence for a time, and Dan shifted his position on the railing.

"It's just that we worry about Bee sometimes," Dan went on. "We used to have a neighbor who did the work around the place. Then he died, and Bee hired you without knowing much about you at all."

"She never asked me nothing," Lonnie said, "and nothing much to tell if she did." He worked silently for a while, but Dan waited him out. At last, encouraged, perhaps, by Dan's apology, Lonnie began to talk: "I never promise how long I'm going to stay, because when the family moves on, I go with 'em. Sometimes I go on ahead to scare up the work, sometimes I don't. Every summer, see, we start down at Havre de Grace and travel north, following the river. Get as far as Mt. Wolf, and we stop there for a time, working the lettuce farms thereabouts. We go north to Lake Otsego, working the orchards, and then start down the other side. Only this year the lettuce crop, it weren't so good, so I come on over here to work for Bee."

"Then it must take a long time to get home of an evening."

Lonnie studied Dan cautiously for a moment, then went on vigorously polishing the blades. "It's not so bad. My dad drives me over of a morning in the truck—lets me off on the road down by the river and I hike the rest of the way. He picks me up at night. Sometimes I stop off in the woods going home and swim in the creek. I like it better over on this side."

"You all work the fields—sisters too?"

"Used to, till Gabe went off." Again the intense eyes focused on Dan suspiciously, as though gauging the amount of trust. Then, "He joined the army last September. We was in Maryland, settled down for the winter so that Gabe and Nancy—she's the youngest—could go to school. All them recruiter people come to the high school, with all that talk of education and advancement. 'See the world, serve your country,' they said. And Gabe tries on a soldier's hat and likes what he sees. Two weeks later, he left school and was off; the day he turned seventeen, he was a soldier."

Lonnie put down the rag and sat back on his heels, resting against the wall. "I don't know, it got to me some way—people coming in like that and breaking up the family. I didn't talk much to anybody for a long time after that, just shut it all up inside myself."

Dan stared, listening to the story. Life at that moment seemed to be a revolving wheel, and he was in the middle of it, watching the same cycles go by again and again.

"Every time I lie down at night I think about him," Lonnie went on, "how the kid's not even shaving yet, and he's carrying a gun. He don't even know who the Asians are or where they're at, but if they send him off, he'll have to fight 'em." He opened his lips and a long sigh escaped that seemed to have scraped the bottom of his chest, and his hands hung limp where the wrists rested on his knees.

"Sometimes it helps to talk—to get it out," Dan said finally.

"Yeah. That's what I decided. No use taking it out on the rest of the family. Oriole, she cried over it. It wasn't only me that was hurting."

The name—the sound of it, the syllables, the face it conjured up. . . . Dan sat without moving, without breathing, almost.

"Oriole—she's the older of your sisters?"

"Yeah, it's me, then Oriole, then Gabe, then Nancy. . . . Used to be a granny that went about with us, but she's gone."

This time Dan let his eyes rest on Lonnie's without glancing away, let the words come without rehearsing them first: "I know you, Lonnie, from somewhere. You were right when you said you had seen me before."

Lonnie returned the gaze. "I was afraid, when I found you lying there in the cellar, that maybe you had the sickness. . . ."

"What sickness?"

Lonnie did not answer him directly. "It was the way you looked at me when you woke up, like you maybe thought you were supposed to be somewhere else, and couldn't remember how you got where you was. That's happened to me before, and I call it the sickness. Times it seems my mind wanders off and I think I've been places and done things that don't make no sense." He waited, making sure that Dan was not laughing at him and then, reassured by Dan's seriousness, went on:

"It's not that my dad won't drive me up here of a morning. I ask him to let me off on the river road so's I can hike through the woods. There's something about it, alone in there among the trees, some feeling I get. . . ." He frowned at his difficulty in describing it. "It's like I belong there, you know? Like I've been some place like that before. Don't make much sense to you, does it?"

"It does, Lonnie, more than you know. Is that all you feel, that you've been in a woods like that before?"

Lonnie turned his face away, as though battling with himself: "That's the good part. But there's more." He turned back again. "Sometimes it's soldiers—soldiers coming, soldiers going. Since Gabe left, I suppose it's on my mind, the army. But it's not a dream, you see. It's not at all like a dream. . . ." He gave up trying to explain and leaned his head against the wall, eyes closed. Dan waited.

"There's times," he said at last, "that I see things clear. I know we can't go on living the way we do, traveling summers up and down the river in a truck. There are times I tell myself maybe Gabe was right, it's time to break away, and then I think of saving enough money to buy Oriole and Nancy bus tickets to someplace out west. California, maybe. I've never been there, but they say it's real nice. Then I think of Gabe leaving and how my mother took it, and I know she couldn't lose her daughters, too. So we just go on, a day at a time, waiting to see what will happen."

Dan felt as though his breath were being cut off from somewhere in his throat, that the tension was rising higher and higher within him and couldn't get out. Was it possible that, had Dan not spent so much time distrusting, Lonnie could have led him to Orlenda? Could she be here somewhere, needing his help, and had he been too blind to see it, too caught up in antagonisms? He had to know.

"What's your sister like—Oriole?"

"She's tall like me—slim. Brown as an Indian." He smiled. "Dark hair, dark eyes. A real pretty girl."

"And Nancy?"

"The same, only smaller."

Dan dug down into the pocket of his jeans and took out the heather. He held it in the palm of his hand and extended it toward Lonnie. "Look, Lonnie. Do you know what this is?"

Lonnie took it, holding it between two fingers. "Looks to me like a weed of some sort."

"It's heather, Lonnie, from the moor."

"Where's that?"

"A long way off—where the soldiers were."

In the shadows of the barn, Lonnie's face seemed to have taken on a grayish-blue cast, and he dropped the heather, withdrawing further and further inside himself. He tipped his head back again against the wall of the barn and once more closed his eyes, as if to shut out everything, Dan included.

"I've not been nowhere else except the river," he said finally, and then, picking up his rag again, he set to work.

"I think I'll drive into town, Bee," Dan told his grandmother after lunch. "Anything you want me to pick up?"

"Not that comes to mind," she answered. "Take you the afternoon and go to a movie or something, Dan."

"I'll see what's playing," he told her and went outside.

The Ford Falcon station wagon was older than Dan by one year. There was a hole in the floor on the right through which he could see the pavement below as he drove down the back roads of Mt. Joy. The gear shift, mounted on the steering column, moved stiffly, like the bones of an old woman; at stop signs, when the car halted, the engine sputtered and Dan had to use the manual choke to keep it going. He nursed it along gently, as though it were Blossom herself, remembering how, as a child, he used to stand on the passenger side where the hole now was, his face pressed against the windshield.

What would he have thought as a young boy, he wondered, had he known something would happen he could not explain? What would he have thought, as a kid in Blossom's car, if he had known that there were things that could hang over his head for a lifetime, questions that might never be resolved? Was it better to be Blossom's age, knowing that while most of your life was past, at least it was yours to keep—no one could take that part of it away from you? Or was it better to be young as he was now, living in the shadow of an illness that could take not only his body but his mind as well?

If it was true what Joe Stanton had told him that night on the moor—that a sensitive person could, in the right place and under the right circumstances, experience something that had happened in the past, what was it that gave Dan that ability? A wish so strong to live in another time or place that he could bodily transport himself? A fear of the future so deep that he wanted out? The steering wheel felt cold beneath his hands.

He did not go into town. He reached the highway along the river and drove toward the bridge. Shadowy bluffs and deep water colored the river a darker green than it was upstream, and rocky promontories jutted out into the channel further down as it narrowed, the current flowing even faster. At the very end of the river, at its sand-lined mouth, where whippoorwills called in the salt-tide marshes, was the place called Job's Hole that Bee had told him about. He thought of it now. An underground passage, she had said, so deep it had no bottom.

He remembered how, as a boy in Bee's cellar, he would send out his name and address on little slips of paper in plastic medicine bottles—letting them float out the opening in the wall. Sometimes he would run along outside, following them until he could go no further. Once he received a postcard from a woman in Virginia saying she had found one of the bottles next to her boat. Had it followed the current down the bay, he mused now, or had it been sucked into the blackness of the hole and carried to Virginia through the passage?

He was surprised to find that in spite of the cool air blowing in through the car window, there was perspiration on his forehead. He turned onto the bridge and crossed over, going south, then headed for Mt. Wolf.

The trees were dense on the other side, more foreboding. Dan turned his attention to the sky again. A storm was definitely coming up. He wondered if he could be back before it rolled in.

He wanted to find Lonnie's sister. He was convinced that if he saw her, he would know whether the similarities were merely coincidence. If she gave any sign of recognition, if she smiled even, the way Jasper's sister had smiled, he would know the girl was Orlenda.

Entering York County, read a sign, and it seemed itself an omen. He drove along Route 24, passing a dead, gray-barked tree covered with climbing vines, its white branches scrabbling at the sky like a crab's claws. Further along the hilly road, maneuvering around curves, he passed a small one-room school of red brick, half-buried in the earth, like the moss-covered barrels in Bee's cellar.

A sudden fear swelled up in his chest that he should not have come—that Orlenda might not be as he had thought, that this was a day, perhaps, for burying delusions. He gripped the wheel tighter and went on.

Crossing over a creek, he came into the Borough of Mt. Wolf. It was small, with old, shingled houses, a barbershop, a factory, a railroad. . . . He drove down Center Street, rounded the block, and then drove back again, stopping finally to get out and wander down the sidewalk. Someone here should know.

He found himself passing an antique shop. Perhaps it was the smell of it—the musty warmth of old fabric and polished pine—or perhaps because the door was open, that Dan went in. It was dark and cluttered, with tall highboys of cherrywood standing row to row along one wall, clocks and mirrors and deep brown oil paintings around the rest of the room. There did not seem to be anyone there, no voice, no footsteps. And then something moved, an old man who had been standing so still in the shadows that Dan must have thought him inanimate.

He came winding his way through the chairs and tables and benches, until at last he stood there in his maroon sweater beside Dan, his watery eyes pink. He seemed much too small for the massive furniture about him.

"Yes?"

"I wonder if you could help me," Dan began. "I'm looking for the Dawson family. They're travelers—migrants, I guess—and I'd heard they were staying for a while in Mt. Wolf."

There was no sign of recognition in the pink eyes. The frail man slowly pulled out a handkerchief and dabbed occasionally at his lids. "Why might you be wanting to see them?"

"I'm a friend of Lonnie Dawson's. It's rather important that I find them."

The old man studied him, dabbed at his tongue with the handkerchief, and then stuffed it back in his pocket.

"Where you from?"

"Mt. Joy, across the river. My name's Dan Roberts."

Still the old man scrutinized him, and it was a long time before he answered. "Strange, you know, you should be looking them up. 'Twas a man in here just this morning asking about them."

"There was?"

"A brash man. Didn't like him, myself. Don't like to be told what to do, you see, I like to be asked."

"Did you tell him where they were?"

Slowly the old face began to smile, like a crinkled piece of paper beginning to unfold, expand. "I told him, all right. I said the Dawsons were through here a few weeks ago and like as not down to Havre de Grace by now."

"But that's heading the wrong way," Dan said. "They go north."

The man laughed this time, and the handkerchief came out of his pocket again. "Now *you* know that, and *I* know that, but the man with all them questions don't know that."

Dan began to smile.

The old man turned serious again. "There's trouble in that family, I'm afraid. Don't know what it is, and the man didn't tell me, but looked to me like he had papers of some sort on 'em."

"If they're in trouble," Dan said quickly, "if there's anything I can do. . . ."

"I think I just might believe you," the old man said. "Not that I'm especially eager to do the migrants a favor, but I'm not of a mind not to, neither. Some folks hereabouts, though, they get nervous, you know, when the migrants come through. But they've never done me no harm. I look at it this way: if it's bad news them papers was all about, well, it'll follow 'em till it catches up, and the least I can do for 'em is put it off for a while."

"Can you tell me where I'll find them?"

The old man took Dan's elbow and steered him back to the door. "I'm not exactly sure myself, but it used to be they'd camp just on the edge of town. Now you go back that way. . . ." He pointed down the road. "And you keep going till you cross the railroad. 'Bout a mile beyond, you'll see an old gate that's only half-standing, and you drive right through there and across the field, on around the cemetery, and it's somewhere back among the pines that the Dawsons set up camp. I've never been there myself. Just heard say."

"I'm really grateful," Dan said, starting down the steps.

"Well, maybe you'll find 'em, maybe you won't," the old man said after him. "Like following the current of a river, isn't it? Here today, gone the next; not the sort you can lay a hand on."

Dan went back to the car, and the first drops of cold rain hit his face, washing off the perspiration that beaded his forehead. He drove in the direction that the man had pointed, crossed the railroad, turned in at the gate, and headed for the pine trees beyond. His heart pounded wildly at the thought that he might find her, this Oriole, the brown-skinned girl whom he had left on the moor. What would he say if she was there? How would he explain his coming? His eyes strained for the sight of a truck. But the road seemed to end at the cemetery, so he got out and walked among the grave markers, his eyes on the trees ahead.

The clearing was there, and the remains of a camp, just as the old man had said. But there was no truck, no people, no clothes drying on the bushes, no pot hanging above the fire.

Dan knelt down and held his hands over the ashes as Joe Stanton had done on the moor. He felt nothing. Then he stood up and kicked at the coals with his boot. A red spark appeared and burned out. Then another.

He looked around quickly, his heart racing. They *were* here, just recently. He walked about the clearing, kicking at things on the ground, searching. . . . Fresh tire tracks in the long grass led to the woods beyond, then disappeared abruptly in the dry bark and pine needles. The anticipation he had felt before turned to dread once again. They had obviously left in a great hurry. Something had happened. Something about the man with the papers. . . .

He walked into the woods a way, but saw nothing. From somewhere off in the distance, he heard a horse whinny, then there was silence. He wondered whether he should go on, or go back to the farm and find Lonnie—tell him what the clerk in the antique store had said. He took another step and a group of birds rose suddenly from a clump of tall grass and went flying to the lowest branch of a nearby tree. And there they sat, looking down at him: magpies.

The dread came over him: the familiar heaviness in his lungs; the tingling of his hands; the rapid, shallow breathing; the sweat. There was not just one magpie about; there were many. He turned and went back through the cemetery, among the crumbling tombstones, where tall grass, long unmowed, protected the dead from the living. The names seemed to rise up from the markers and come at him: Higgins, Sandison, Kauffman, Bart. . . .

And then he saw a hump of earth without a marker at all off on the edge of the field, belonging more to the trees than the cemetery itself. He paused, his heart pounding. The rain came down on him and he scarcely noticed. He walked over and knelt down.

It was not a fresh grave—had been there, perhaps, for several years. It was overgrown with grass and weeds, and the thorn bush, growing on top, was shaggy and untrimmed. But there, twisted round and round among its branches, impaled on the thorns, was a once-red piece of yarn, long since faded, now only the faintest pink.

Dan stood up, backing off, and then made a run for the car. He tortured himself as he drove home; back the road he had come, past the half-buried schoolhouse and the dead tree scrabbling at the sky. Why had he come here? Why hadn't he told Lonnie about the Roman soldiers and a girl named Orlenda and how Dan wanted very much to help Lonnie's sister, if only he knew where to find her? Why this wild goose chase to a place across the river when the one person who knew her waited there on the other side?

Rain lashed furiously at the windshield as he crossed

the bridge again at Wrightsville, and gusts of wind buffeted the side of the station wagon, forcing him to grip the wheel more tightly for control. To his left, the Susquehanna drank in the downpour that pounded upon her surface and the strange light from the gray sky made shadows behind the large rocks that loomed up from the water.

For the first time since Dan had returned from York, for the first time since he had discovered the awful family secret that seemed to paralyze his father and immobilize Dan himself at times with feelings of hopelessness, he had discovered—with Orlenda—a rage to live, a reason to exist, a purpose to the comings and goings of his life. He could do nothing to ward off what might lie in wait for him at some distant time, but he could do something now for her. Wherever it was he had left her, she was counting on him to come back, and he felt as though his mind, his will, his strength, his muscles, his emotions were geared to that alone; he must find her.

He turned off onto the side road that meandered among the farms, following Little Donegal Creek as it tumbled past him, swollen from the cloudburst. Trees, already heavy with summer foliage, hung even lower with the weight of the water, humbled by the force of the winds.

Blossom's farmhouse stood starkly against the black sky, the barn looming up behind it, taller still, and the clouds seemed to roll across its roof, up one side and down the other. There was no lightning, no thunder—only the relentless surge of a storm that would not break.

Dan leaped from the car and ran to the door of the house, using his shoulder, once inside, to close it fast against the wind. Ordinarily, in a storm such as this, Lonnie would be in the kitchen with Bee, her teakettle whistling, and he would be hunched over the table, a plate of biscuits before him. The kitchen, however, was empty. There were no wet footprints on the floor, no sign of crumbs on the table.

"Bee?" Dan called, and went through the rooms searching. In the front hallway he found the door to his grandmother's bedroom ajar and looked in, but Bee was not taking her afternoon nap; the room was empty. He started for the back door when suddenly he heard it, the unmistakable call of his name. The cold began this time at the soles of his feet, as though an icy vapor were seeping up between the floorboards and seizing him by the ankles.

"Dan." The voice came again, and it belonged unmistakably to Ambrose.

Dan walked to the door of the cellar and flung it open, but he did not go down.

"The coin, Dan. . . ." the voice repeated from the direction of the spring. "The Roman denarius."

"Forget it," Dan called. He realized, more certain than ever, that he was master here, that the face in the water was trapped forever beneath the surface unless he spoke aloud the gypsy's name in its presence. He had no need of Ambrose now; it was Lonnie who would lead him to Orlenda.

"You don't recognize me, perhaps?" the voice continued.

"Oh, but I do."

"You've forgotten my name?"

Dan was positive now. "No, I know it too well."

"Well, then. . . ."

"That's much too easy. I won't give you the coin for nothing. I want my belt."

"I offered to pay. . . ."

"I don't want money. If I'm to have nothing of yours, you are to keep nothing of mine."

"I don't have the belt, Dan," the voice said, and seemed to be growing softer, making Dan come down a few steps in order to hear it.

"Where is it?"

"Lost."

"I don't believe you."

The voice continued, softer still. "I threw it away in anger, but I'll pay for the coin. Eight pounds, eh? No? Ten pounds. . . ."

Dan was halfway down the stairs and determined to go no further; he had other things to do; he had to get out to the barn and see Lonnie. "I want something else," he told the voice. "I want to meet once more with Orlenda."

He expected an argument, a reply, a lie, even. Instead, he was met with silence. There was nothing more from the spring, except the usual bubbling and trickling of the water, and feeling that he had already lost valuable time, Dan wheeled about and rushed on outside to the barn.

7

H E SPRINTED through the deep puddles, soaked to the skin by the time he reached the barn door. Opening it enough just to squeeze through, so that the wind could not catch it, he pulled it to and latched it from the inside.

"Lonnie?" he called softly, making his way along the dark stalls.

There was a sound of squeaking and scraping from behind the railing and then, from the cow's stall, something white rose up. Dan sucked in his breath, jolted by the sudden specter, and then his muscles relaxed and his shoulders slumped, for it was Blossom.

"Lord, Dan! Make you some noise when you come in, will you? You going to go creeping around the barn like that, you bang a door or something. Like to scare me to death!"

Blossom sank back down on the stool where she had been milking. "Begun to worry about you, out in the storm in that old battle wagon. A gust of wind hit the side of that car and it's like a sail—carry you clear across the river if you're not careful."

"Where's Lonnie?" Dan asked quickly.

Blossom looked up at him for a moment and then went on milking, her old hands moving rhythmically. "He's gone. The way that sky looked about one-thirty, I knew we were in for a blow, so I let him off early. Figured he could hitchhike and get home before the worst of it hit. Don't know where my mind was. Should have had you drive 'im over—least as far as the bridge."

Dan leaned weakly against a post, feeling that something had knocked the wind out of him. How could things turn out so wrong? How could he so easily have missed his chance?

He wheeled about and rushed outside, pushing the door tightly closed behind him, standing against the barn, his face up to the sky, eyes closed, letting the rain pummel him, soak him through.

Would he ever find her? How could he get out of his own cocoon of worry and foreboding if he could not channel it into a concern for someone else? How could he ever prove that he had indeed been somewhere that night he lay in the cellar and that it was not just a sickness in his

166

head? How much better to have the enemy without than within. Better to be pursued by phantoms of the past then phantoms of the mind. Better to know, even, that his life was caught up in a psychic drama he could not understand or explain than to think that his own body had turned traitor. He had indeed been on the moor last night, and he was convinced that Lonnie had been there with him. But now Lonnie was gone. And if there was trouble across the river, as the man in the antique store had thought, Lonnie would probably not be back at all.

He ran into the house and clattered down the stairs to the cellar, bending once more over the spring. And this time the face was waiting for him. The features were so clear, so distinct, that the water was more like window glass, revealing every line, every hair on the gypsy's face. The long nose, wide at the bottom, the shaggy brows, the deep creases about the eyes, the black mustache, mingling with the gray of the beard. . . .

Ambrose had been waiting for him, he knew—biding his time, knowing that Dan would come.

He sank back on his heels, his heart pounding, his face white, the clammy dread surrounding him like a heavy blanket. What he was about to do could not be undone; once beckoned, the spirit was unchained. But it was, Dan knew, his last remaining link with Orlenda, and so he threw back his head and shouted:

"Ambrose! Ambrose Faw!"

Immediately his body felt as though it had been pricked with a thousand icy needles. A wind seemed to sweep through the opening in the wall where the stream ran through; the gentle bubbling sound of the water became more like a crackle, like dry branches giving way under footsteps, and the entire cellar grew darker still in the gloom of the late afternoon.

Dan drew in his breath sharply and looked around, half expecting to see the big man appear behind him. But the face in the water began to blur slightly, then to recede. It grew more and more faint until, where it had been so distinct before, there was only the pebbled bottom of the shallow stream.

In its place there came a silence so profound that it was more terrifying than anything else Dan had experienced; the stream stopped bubbling, the wind stopped blowing; the silence in his own head was so oppressive, so overwhelming, that Dan cried out in terror and was horrified to discover that he could not hear his own voice. And then, just as suddenly, the stream began to bubble again, the wind began to blow, and Dan got shakily to his feet and went back upstairs to the kitchen.

They were coming now, he was sure of it, and he welcomed them with both anticipation and dread. He was stalked as surely as the hunted by the hunter, and yet he was eager for the confrontation, mad to get it over with. The battle was here and now, not some elusive question mark hanging over him in the future.

Had anyone, ever before, he wondered, had to live under such question marks as he—he and his father? During the Black Plague, perhaps. His class had discussed it last year in history, and he could still see the teacher standing there in front of the room saying, "One third the population of Britain was wiped out. *Think* of it. One third the population of Britain." No one knew at the time what caused it, no one knew whether it would pass him by. But it was coming, coming—first one village and then the next. Dan had read about how new crops went unplanted, old ones went unharvested, and fear turned friend against friend.

Yes, that had been the landscape of his mind. He had been unable to reach out for anything, afraid to plan or hope or prepare or dream. There had been times over the past few weeks when he felt that he would be better off staying here in Mt. Joy forever, hidden from view so that people would not be frightened by the lapses of his brain— times also, however, when he felt that he could not bear, even here, the suspense, the uncertainty, could not go on night after night listening for the call in the dark, watching for shadows on the wall, searching the water for faces. Madness, surely.

But now the wait was over. He had called them, and they were coming, and his body—which craved action, movement, response—felt strong.

It was after dinner, when the dishes had been done and cream put out for the cat, that Bee put down the magazine she was reading and looked across at Dan. They had opened the windows wide in the parlor so that the cool night breeze could penetrate the rooms. When the sun rose the next day, hot and heavy, the windows would be closed again to trap the air in. But now, as the curtains flapped, Bee fastened her faded blue eyes on her grandson:

"You didn't go to the movies this afternoon, did you?"

"No, Bee, I just drove around for a while."

"I thought you might. I knew it would upset you, your falling like that in the cellar. I was afraid you might do something foolish."

Dan smiled a little. "Drive into the river or something?"

"Well, it happens. Folks start worrying so about what might happen that they go off and do something really crazy."

"You know what I decided, Bee?" Dan said, wanting to reassure her. "That fear can be as bad as Huntington's disease itself. I could get so frightened, so paralyzed about my chances, that I would be as crippled as if I had it. I could let the fear take over and rob me of everything. I don't want that to happen."

"*Now* you're talking sense," Bee said. "That's the spirit! Lord, if we sat us down and thought of all the things that *might* happen to us, we wouldn't ever get out of bed in the morning."

"The problem isn't knowing what to do, it's knowing how to do it. Telling somebody not to worry is like telling them not to feel any pain. They don't want to feel it, they wish they didn't, but they do, and pretending doesn't make it go away. Sometimes the pain is there, and you've got to deal with it. That's my problem now. I've made up my mind that I won't let the fear take over, but I'm not sure how to stop it."

"You'll work it out, Dan."

"I'll sure give it a good try."

The cold dampness of the earth and the warm air that was blowing in from the west made fog. Dan could see it from his bedroom window, sweeping in over the pasture and mixing with the mist.

Objects in the barnyard appeared and disappeared as the fog rose and fell and went rolling on across the meadow. The barn was there one moment and gone the next, trees came into view and dissolved again. It reminded him of the mist on the moor the morning he had awakened with Orlenda in his arms.

Was it possible that it was all over, what had happened

centuries past? That she had married a Roman soldier, perhaps, and borne his children? Was it possible that she was long since buried, like the old Granny, and her descendants scattered? Or was she waiting for him, somewhere, to come back? He simply could not believe he would never see her again.

He agonized as he thought of her, remembering the scent of her hair and the feel of her skin—the way she had wept that morning at the sound of the battle. Somehow, somewhere, he would find her.

He did not know how long he sat at the window, his feet propped up on the sill, intoxicated by the mist that floated in. But he was conscious finally of how far the moon had risen from where he had seen it last. It was time for sleep.

He had just stepped out in the hall toward the bathroom when he saw a flickering of light on the wall at the bottom of the stairs. He waited, wondering—certain that Blossom had gone to bed. He sniffed at the air, searching for smoke, thinking possibly of a fire somewhere in the rooms below. Finally he turned and hurried softly downstairs and into the parlor.

The light was coming from the kitchen, and he could tell at once it was the flickering light of the kerosene lamp. Perhaps Blossom had gone to the cellar earlier to put some food in the stream and had left the lamp, lit, on the table.

He could hear the squeak of her kitchen rocker, however, so someone was up—someone sitting there in the middle of the floor.

Softly he went through the parlor in his bare feet, feeling his way along in the moonlight that streamed in through the windows. He attracted the attention of the cat, sleeping on the dusty sofa. It jerked up its head and watched Dan pass, its yellow eyes glowing in the darkness.

The door between the kitchen and the parlor was ajar, but swung slightly back and forth as the wind tossed it first one way and then another. The windows were still open, and the parlor curtains flapped vigorously in the night breeze.

He hugged the wall as he approached the door, stepping down gently on the old floorboards to soften the squeak, and stood just outside the kitchen, waiting for another whisper of wind to swing the door open again.

Blossom sat in the rocker, her long white hair hanging loose about her shoulders. She rocked in rhythm, back and forth, back and forth for a minute or so, and then she would stop, sitting motionless, her head cocked sideways as though listening. She had turned her chair so that it was facing the cellar, and the cellar door was open.

Why the sight of it terrified him, Dan did not know. But the fact that she sat and rocked and faced the cellar on this night of all nights seemed more than a coincidence. She was obviously waiting for something, for someone, and each time she stopped, each time she listened, her head seemed to lean forward just a little more, as though on the verge of catching the sound for which she was waiting.

Suddenly he was aware that the rocking had stopped once more and did not resume again. Blossom sat straight up, her neck stiff, head taut.

"Who's there?" she asked, without turning around.

How could she know? Dan wondered. He had made no noise, given no hint. And yet she sat as though she knew he was there at the doorway, watching. Or was she hearing something else—footsteps, perhaps, in the cellar?

At that moment he felt the chill again on his legs, a clammy breeze on the back of his neck, and then, along with it, the dread. He had a sudden terrifying feeling that they were not alone, and that it was this person to whom Blossom was speaking.

Something brushed against his legs, and then the cat went by him, scraping its back on the edge of the door. It padded on out to the kitchen, where it paused a moment before leaping onto Bee's lap.

"Eh? So it's you, then," the old woman said, and lifted the cat in her arms. The rocking began again, and the cat lay still, its yellow eyes shining there in the shadows.

✳ ✳ ✳

Dan lay in bed that night too tense for sleep. Who was she waiting for? For Lonnie to come back? Her great-grandfather, the tinker? For spirits he knew nothing of? Or was she, in an old woman's ritual, merely opening the door each night to death, should it care to come and take her, showing the peace she had made within herself? Was it possible that Blossom, too, had links with her past—that Blossom had been places she never talked about? Could she, like the old gypsy granny, have a gift of flowing through past and present and future and was giving it to Dan—his inheritance?

At what point did the past end and the present begin, or the present leave off and the future take over? Each day that passed meant more history heaped upon itself, and the future—tenuous thing that it was—lay like a silver thread, a question mark, over all that was to be.

Whatever, the dread that Dan had felt in the rooms below had been replaced with a strange kind of exhilaration. There would be no more waiting, no more wondering. Ambrose, he knew, was on the way. Dan still had the coin, the Roman denarius, safe in the watchband, secure around his wrist. He would not give it up until he had met once more with Orlenda. He got out of bed suddenly and, taking the small piece of heather he had found in his hair, stuck it in a crack in his window frame, facing the woods and the river beyond.

*** ※ ***

Close after the hour of midnight, when traffic over the bridge had dwindled to an occasional driver—a shift worker on his way home to bed—an old green truck crossed the Susquehanna. It was a makeshift affair, with fenders of a different vintage and an entire door replaced with one of red. It was smaller than a delivery truck, larger than a van—more like a school bus, actually, except there were fewer windows.

Those that there were had curtains on them, each of a different pattern, and at one of the windows there was a small pot of African violets that looked almost black under the night sky. The truck moved slowly, not more than fifteen miles an hour, for trotting along behind it was a gray horse, its hoofs clanking against the floor of the bridge, a strange counterpart to the hum of the truck's engine. There was a man on the horse, but his features were indistinguishable in the shadows.

Beneath the bridge, the Susquehanna tumbled swiftly, swelled by the rain of the afternoon. Rocks that had been only half-hidden at two o'clock were now barely visible, and there was a dim roar as the river chased itself, one ripple following on the edge of another, until they collided at the boulders that waited downstream, dissolving in a froth of white water.

When the green truck and the horse behind reached

the north side of the bridge, they turned left along the river road. Ordinarily, at this season, they would have been following the river on the other side. But on this night, under cover of darkness, they had crossed over.

Soon they turned again on a smaller road and then, further on, a smaller one still. They followed the path of Little Donegal Creek until they reached a place where the fence was down—had been, for many years. Here they followed a lane that wound about among the trees, leading deeper and deeper into the woods. When they came to a small clearing and the truck stopped, the horse waited, its head down. The rider slid off and, leading the horse, one hand on its mane, took it down to the gully where it stood with its forelegs in the water, neck stretched, gulping slowly. The man patted its side and stroked it and crooned in a language all his own.

The door at the back of the truck swung open, and a figure stepped out into the moonlight—a blur of orange and purple. Shapes moved in slow motion, muted flashes of color, and then they were shadows once more. There was the sound of a small child's voice, a sleepy question, a man's gentle response, the squeak of a window as it opened, the flop of a blanket being shaken, and then, one by one, the figures disappeared. A man stretched out on the long grass and lay still, and at last there were no more questions, no more answers—only the soft crunch in the horse's mouth as it grazed in the coolness of the wood.

The air was growing warmer still, despite the hour, and the mist that Dan had seen from his window earlier that evening had become even thicker. The south pasture, which was the only thing separating the woods from Blossom's house, was completely hidden in fog, and if Dan had looked out now, he could have seen nothing. Nothing at all.

But the truck had come, and the gray horse with it, and there were several hours left before dawn.

FOOTPRINTS AT THE WINDOW

H E NO LONGER heard his name, he heard footsteps. They came when he least expected them, and Dan could not tell if they were above or below or beside him. But they were there, like a heartbeat—now fainter, now more distinct—and then they would disappear altogether, only to come again when his mind was on other things.

"There're gypsies about," Blossom said that morning over her white tea—white, she called it, because she took it with cream. "I've seen their smoke over the woods—just a wisp, but it's there."

Dan watched her from across the table. Like the flat stump of an old tree, her face seemed to have a line for every year of her life. "How can you tell they're gypsies?" he asked.

"I know the signs." Blossom clicked her teeth. "There was a rooster missing yesterday—the red bantam with the lame leg. They do that, you know. If they take something from you, they'll not pick the finest, but something with a defect, just to salve their conscience. They're not stealing, mind you, just thinning things out a bit." The laugh lines at the corners of her eyes deepened.

"Have you seen anyone about?"

"Not yet."

He stood on the back porch and looked out over the south pasture. Just as Blossom had said, smoke rose up over the woods beyond and hovered there against the blue of the sky, a thin curl, like a question mark.

He would not go searching them out—not yet, anyway. As long as he had the coin, the ancient Roman denarius, secure in the slit of his watchband, the gypsies would come to him, he was sure of it. Ever since Nat had traded it to him in York last spring for his belt, the Faws had been wild to get it back. He would wait.

Lonnie, the young man whom Bee had hired for the summer, was gone. There was work from the time Dan got up in the morning until he fell exhausted into bed at night—clipping shrubs, chopping wood, digging, hoeing—mindless chores that taxed his strength but not his head. Lonnie had left early the day of the storm and not come back. It did not bother Blossom particularly. She had raised children of her own, and she knew when a young man was getting restless, she said, eager to be off and about, by now he was far up the river. But Dan stood at the door, watching the smoke, and wasn't so sure.

"They've been through here before, the gypsies?" he asked later as he hoed with his grandmother in the garden.

Blossom bent down and rummaged through the green of the cucumber leaves. Her face glowed in the heat of the sun, and even her scalp was pink beneath the sparse strands of white hair.

"Every now and then," she replied, and straightened up slowly, one hand to her back. "Used to be I'd see them right often—when I was a young bride—every summer or two. The children would knock on my door selling violets and snowdrops or watercress. But now there are long stretches—years, even—when I don't see them at all, and just when I've decided they're gone for good, there's their smoke once more." She squinted toward the woods in the distance. "I don't mind them taking my rooster; it's comforting to an old soul like me to have them return, like one of earth's cycles, you know. There're times I've suspected that on a particularly wet night, they've come up across the south pasture and spent the night in my barn, but I don't care a bit. Only once did I take them to task."

Carrying the cucumbers in her apron, Blossom shuffled over to the bench under the beech tree and sat down, smiling to herself. "I'd left my wash on the line overnight, and first thing I saw the next morning were two gypsy women looking my dresses over. One woman was in red—a long skirt down to the ankles—and the other in blue, and they were fingering my good yellow dress with the purple flowers, feeling it, you know, to test the cloth. I stuck my head out the window and called, 'Not my yellow dress, ladies. Help yourself to the green one down there on the end if you like, but the yellow one I'm wearing to Harrisburg next Sunday.'"

She chuckled. "And you know, they bowed—curtsied, sort of, the way they do in England to the Queen—and took the green dress with a 'Thank you, mum.' The next morning I found me a bouquet of flowers on my doorstep, and by the time I got them in and on the table, I realized they were my own geraniums." Both she and Dan laughed out loud. Blossom wiped her eyes in merriment. "That's why I like to see the smoke above the trees. Like old friends, that's what the gypsies are, here to pay me a visit."

When would they come, then—that night? Dan wondered, listening to a light rain fall as he and Blossom ate their supper. Would the gypsies be content this time to sleep in the barn or pick the flowers or go off with another chicken? Or would they come inside and up to his room, looking for the Roman denarius?